Portraits of the Past

Portraits of the Past

Richard Muir

MICHAEL JOSEPH
London

MICHAEL JOSEPH LTD

Published by the Penguin Group
27 Wrights Lane, London W8 5TZ England
Viking Penguin Inc. 40 West 23rd Street, New York, New York 10010, USA
Penguin Books Australia Ltd. Ringwood, Victoria, Australia
Penguin Books Canada Ltd. 2801 John Street, Markham, Ontario, Canada L3R 1H4
Penguin Books (NZ) Ltd 182–190 Wairau Road, Auckland 10, New Zealand

Penguin Books Ltd, Registered Offices: Harmondsworth, Middlesex, England

First published in Great Britain 1989
Text Copyright © Richard Muir 1989

Typeset by Goodfellow & Egan (Phototypesetting) Ltd, Cambridge
Made and printed in Great Britain by Butler & Tanner Ltd, Frome

A CIP catalogue record for this book is available from the British Library

ISBN 0 7181 3181 9

ACKNOWLEDGEMENTS

I should like to express my gratitude for the generous assistance provided by the following people and institutions: Graham Cadman, Mrs Courtney of the National Museum of Wales, A.H.A. Hogg, Michael Jones, Jorvik Viking Centre, Simon Manby, R.J. Mercer, Peter E. Ryder, Maggi Solly, David Vale, Martin Wildgoose.

Contents

Acknowledgements iv

Introduction 1

1 Back to the Beginnings: 200,000 years ago 4
2 At Home in the Forest 13
3 Temples in a Shrinking Forest 20
4 The Patchwork Countryside of the Bronze Age 34
5 Fighting and Farming in the Iron Age 43
6 The Roman Experience 57
7 The Time of Arthur: the Darkness that Followed 74
8 The Time of Alfred: the Hidden Revolution 86
9 A Trip Through Domesday England 103
10 Robin Hood's England 119
11 The Tortured Realm of Pilgrims and Piers Plowman 135
12 The Elizabethan Countryside Revealed 148
13 Rob Roy's Scotland 166
14 The Georgian Era: The Privatisation of the Countryside 171

Index 183

Introduction

THIS IS A BOOK ABOUT the appearance of the countryside – its vegetation, farming patterns, settlement and habitations – in former times. Not long ago the look of lost landscapes was an apparently insoluble puzzle. However, in the course of the last two or three decades our understanding of the past has, largely as a result of new archaeological techniques, increased enormously. We are scarcely more than a generation removed from a time when it was thought that Iron Age people lived in pits in the ground – these holes now being recognised as their grain storage pits. And there are still plenty of schoolteachers at work who regard Saxon England as a sea of virgin forest, even though we now know that the assault on the woodland began around 7,000 years ago. Wherever unspoiled countryside survives today it is likely to display an inheritance of features derived from many different eras of the past. The woods might have been managed since medieval times; the eighteenth-century field patterns might be superimposed upon the traces of feudal farming; and these in turn might mask prehistoric field banks – and so on until eventually facets of a dozen different ages of endeavour are recognised.

A whole range of specialist techniques has helped to open our eyes to the scenes which were viewed by our distant forebears. Radio-carbon dating enables us to locate organic remains in time – or at least to know that the item concerned perished within certain time brackets. But then from the study of dendrochronology or tree-ring dating it emerged that radio-carbon dates became progressively too 'young' as one went back in time. So the radio-carbon dates quoted here have been recalibrated according to a curve based on dendrochronology. Since trees grow at different rates in different seasons according to factors like warmth and rainfall each sequence of tree rings produces a distinct 'fingerprint'. Thus growth rings in cores taken from the timbers of an old house can be matched against growth patterns derived from dated timbers from the same general vicinity, and the house timbers can then be dated so precisely that one discovers the exact year in which the trees incorporated in the house were felled. Problems arise, however, when buildings incorporate timbers reused from earlier buildings – formerly quite a common practice.

The most valuable information about the vegetation of former environ-

I

ments derives from ancient pollen grains. Most pollen-producing plants produce grains which are of a quite distinctive form. These grains are armoured by a tough coating which allows them to survive for thousands of years in suitably damp conditions. Thus, experts are able to take pollen samples from buried and datable peat layers and deduce which plants were present in ancient environments. It is not possible to create an absolutely exact picture and allowance must be made for various factors – for example, the lime is not a heavy producer of pollen and may be under-represented in a pollen sample. But the science does allow one to recognise early farming episodes from the arrival of pollen from weeds of cultivation, while the discovery of large quantities of ivy pollen at one site led to the suggestion that Mesolithic people were gathering ivy as fodder for semi-domesticated reindeer. Other durable relics, like snail shells and the wing cases of beetles, are also scrupulously studied and produce evidence of past environments: certain invertebrates flourish in woodland settings, others in and around ditches and so on.

Archaeological excavation has increasingly become an exacting and painstaking science. Generally, however, the excavations tell about the below-ground features of buildings. Excavation of the silt-filled holes which once carried posts produces evidence of the ground plans of buildings and may allow intelligent guesses to be made about construction. Usually, however, the above-ground appearance of the building is conjectural and in the drawings of the Saxon building excavated at Cowdery's Down (p. 80) we see three different interpretations.

Graveyards of many ages have been excavated and the human remains have been subjected to careful medical scrutiny. We learn about the stature of people – the survival of various suits of armour made for boys may be responsible for the common misconception that our forebears were very short. We also learn about life expectancy and the diseases which afflicted our ancestors, discovering, for example, the widespread horrors of tooth decay and arthritis, or that many Neolithic men bore battle wounds. Less glamorous has been the excavation of privies and cesspits. These tell us about the medieval diet and that our ancestors were likely to have suffered from tapeworms and other parasites.

While the archaeologist can tell us about what he or she has found and not dwell on what has not been discovered, the artist working on reconstruction drawings cannot gloss over the gaps in knowledge. One cannot leave a void because of doubts about how a roof was built or where windows were placed. A measure of imagination and understanding is required as well, and sometimes a morsel of courage. Mistakes will be made, but there is no better way of conveying a picture of the past than via a carefully executed reconstruction drawing.

With the dawning of the historical age written information becomes available. All too often, however, the scribes or recorders either did not consider it their brief to describe the look of the land or else they decided that everyone was quite familiar with the setting and did not need any written description. Consequently hints must often be gleaned from sources like land charters, laws or poems.

Some Saxon and a fair selection of medieval drawings have survived, but the great breakthrough in our quest for a detailed understanding of former countrysides arrived with the appearance of estate maps in Elizabethan times. There were also, of course, landscape paintings or paintings with landscape as a backdrop. These may not be entirely reliable, for scenery was perceived according to the fashions of the times. A mildly rolling English countryside could be turned into a dramatic parody of a fashionable Tuscan landscape. Indeed, it is strange how perceptions change: some eighteenth-century arbiters of taste produced scathing accounts of the now much-loved countrysides of the Lake District and the Cotswolds.

In writing the text I have attempted to do rather more than provide a commentary on the illustrations, though these must occupy the centre of the stage. The deep debt to many contributors is expressed in the list of acknowledgements.

CHAPTER ONE

Back to the Beginnings: 200,000 years ago

WHEN A PERSON WHO IS aware and thoughtful goes a-rambling we can be pretty sure that, as the scenic images seep from eye to brain, some historical visions and puzzles will begin to ferment. What did this rural nook look like when that stag-headed oak was just an acorn? What views were revealed to the medieval masons as they clambered up the scaffolding of the rising church spire? Did the Romans pass this way and were there wagons and taverns and road gangs to ease their journeys? Was there really a gallows on Gallows Crag, a beacon on Toot Hill and a mill on Wind Hill mound? An awareness that, under the spur of human endeavour, scenery is forever changing has existed for countless years. Nobody has expressed this knowledge more tellingly than the Elizabethan poet, Michael Drayton (1563–1631):

> The ridge and furrow show that once the crooked plough
> Turned up the grassy turf, where oaks are rooted now:
> And at this hour we see the share and coulter tear
> The corn-bearing glebe, where sometimes forests were.

For some specialist historians the past is to be found fossilised within archive vaults, where dusty ledgers, stained parchments and fading charters all whisper messages about the high enterprises and parochial trivia of yesteryear. But for many more the past is a picture pastiche which glows, flickers and fades as we step beyond the bounds of memory and struggle to imagine familiar places as they might have existed a hundred, five hundred or five thousand years ago. Today we are assisted in our historical musings by modern archaeological skills and technologies, so it may not be too difficult to write an accurate and detailed description of a village deserted three thousand years ago. However, the artist or film-maker would find such data incomplete (where *exactly* did each wayside bush stand, what colour were the people's robes, what language did they speak and with which accent?).

As we slip down the spiral of history we are confronted by changes

4

coming from many quarters. Not only the people, their costumes and customs, homes, equipment and machines change, but so too do the vegetation, the wildlife, the climate and even the configuration of the country. Slide too swiftly down the British spiral and you might perish in a polar desert, a coral sea or a morass of scorching lava.

Any historical story must have a beginning and here it would be apt to start with an exploration of the setting occupied by the very first Briton. Sadly we will never know just who this man or woman was, or quite when he or she arrived during one of the prolonged interglacial interludes of mildness which separated the harsh glacial eras. But we can imagine a small pioneering family band of hunters and gatherers plodding across the flat marshy landbridge from the continent and arriving in south-eastern England without knowing they had arrived, though probably feeling rather lost.

A fossilised carnium fragment discovered at Swanscombe, south of the Thames – now sandwiched between Dartford and Northfleet – is our introduction to the first English person of whom we have any skeletal relic. It suggests an individual who stood at an early stage in the evolution of our own *Homo sapiens* line from the successful, widespread but heavily browed

The hunting life of 'Swanscombe Man' by Maurice Wilson. Perhaps these early occupants of southern Britain would have been naked on warm summer days but at other times they must have worn clothes tailored from animal skins. By courtesy of the British Museum (Natural History).

5

and jowled *Homo erectus* lineage (which includes Pekin Man and Java Man). *Homo erectus* almost certainly evolved in Africa and it now seems possible that every human alive today is descended from a single African mother. Our Neanderthal cousins would arrive later, with their massively muscled physiques adapted to arduous and perhaps aimless ramblings as they pursued big game across frozen vastnesses. They would perish along with the waning ice.

To make a rendezvous with our Swanscombe predecessors, we must travel back in time for 200,000 years and then a bit more. Should we pack snow shoes and arctic survival gear or tee-shirts and sun hats? Actually, the proverbial stout shoes and a jumper will serve, for the climate is temperate and not unlike the mild oceanic conditions of today.

At the time of our arrival the ancestral Thames flows to the south of the modern river. There are, of course, no field ditches, locks, embankments or barrages to control and pacify the river, so it flows freely and recklessly, sometimes splitting into a series of braided channels. If we walk along the gravelly shore of such a channel, eyes down and carefully scanning, we will surely find a site where animals have been skinned and butchered. Amongst the gory relics of the kill are discarded tools. There are 'handaxes': carefully flaked flints roughly the size and shape of a very large, flattened and sharply pointed pear. Handaxes, used with their rounded end grasped firmly in the palm, seem to have been general-purpose tools used for cleaving, crushing, stabbing and digging.

They are not the first tools to be made by man in Britain and were we to dig down into the river gravels for just a few feet then we would discover the products of a different and rather earlier flint industry. Its artefacts do not comprise elegantly shaped handaxes but flints with sharply chipped edges which served as choppers and angular flakes of flint used for slicing meat and scraping hides. The makers of these tools hunted this area in an earlier stage of the same interglacial era, but as yet not a trace of their mortal remains has been discovered.

The countryside bordering the river exists as open grassland, while the floodplain in the higher land is cloaked in woodland. Here and there we see ash, scorched roots and fire-blackened soil. Was it lightning that caused the woods to burn, allowing the grazings to expand? Or had man already begun deliberately to modify his environment, creating open pastures and hunting ranges and launching the revolutions of change which would one day produce fields and freeways, towns and telegraph poles and all the paraphernalia of the modern world? Certainly the abundance of camp sites and discarded tools in this Thames-side area suggests that human groups, whether native or regular visitors from what is now the continent, are quite numerous and successful.

6

At first the woodlands do not seem too unfamiliar, and we recognise alder, hazel, elm, lime and yew growing within the oak-dominated forest. There are also familiar faces amongst the fauna. Animals which still flourish in Britain include red deer and roe deer, mountain hare, the woodmouse, common shrew and several voles. The wildcat and pine marten, which are now extremely rare, are quite frequently glimpsed and there are also fallow deer and rabbits, both of which became extinct in Britain and were reintroduced by the Normans. Amongst the animals which were present more than 200,000 years ago and became extinct in Britain during historical times are the beaver, the wolf and the wild boar. A giant and heavily-horned ox, the 'aurochs' is extinct today, though Corpus Christi College, Cambridge, has owned an aurochs drinking horn since 1352, and the Sutton Hoo Saxon ship burial included a similar drinking horn, perhaps imported from Scandinavia. This probably came from a continental survivor, the beast having been hunted out in Britain perhaps 2,500 years ago. The last aurochs of all is believed to have died in a Polish park in 1627 but the survival of aurochs' genes in 'primitive' cattle might allow breeding back to produce beasts closely resembling the wild ox.

But there are other animals roaming the ancient woods and pastures which one would certainly not expect to meet on any English country walk, past or present. If the most surprising is the Barbary ape (now commonly

An aurochs as reconstructed by Maurice Wilson/Sally Wilson. The Illustrated London News Picture Library.

associated with the colony preserved at Gibraltar), the most imposing is the long-extinct straight-tusked elephant. Much larger than a woolly mammoth, it stands a good 11 ft (3.4 m) tall, with enormous tusks which brush the ground. Perhaps man hunted this magnificent animal to extinction: at Lehringer, in Lower Saxony, the skeleton of a straight-tusked elephant was discovered with an 8-ft (2.4-m) spear of yew lodged in its ribs. Similar spears were carried by our handaxe makers. One or perhaps two kinds of rhinoceros existed: the species known as *Dicerorhinus hemitoechus* had two horns, was around 10 ft (3 m) from nose to tail and would rather have resembled the black and the white rhinos of Africa; *Dicerorhinus kirchbergensis* was slightly smaller and may or may not have been present.

While the wise time traveller would keep downwind of the elephant and rhino every possible care would be taken to avoid two formidable predators, the lion and the cave bear. Comparable in size to the surviving brown bear, the cave bear was feared and venerated by ancient hunting communities in Europe: ritual collections of its bones and skulls have been found in several cave complexes occupied by Neanderthal hunters. Amongst the cave-living classes the first step in home-making must have been the daunting one of evicting an extremely large, angry and ferocious sitting tenant ('Just pop into the cave, dear, and see if there are any more inside').

While these animals or their not-too-distant cousins can be seen in zoos or, preferably, on wild-life movies, there was one other inhabitant of the ancient Thames-side scene which would have appeared to be the ultimate

8

in outlandish appearance; its name, the giant deer, hardly does justice to the beast. It stood around 10 ft (3 m) tall and carried an amazing set of moose-style antlers with a span of ten or more feet. The antlers seem to have been male status symbols rather than weapons and they would have greatly impeded swift movement through woodland. The giant deer was present in various interglacial eras prior to its extinction and the development of the most showy and spreading headgear seems to have been associated with life in open country, while upswept antlers characterised stags inhabiting wooded country.

Swanscombe was by no means the only part of England occupied at this time, for other roughly contemporaneous communities are known to have existed elsewhere near London: near Hitchin, near Ipswich, in Essex; at a lakeshore site at Hoxne, in Suffolk; and on higher ground in the Chilterns and the Wiltshire Downs. Wild horses were probably the main prey of the human hunters and aurochs, deer, elephant and rhino were also hunted. Since lush vegetation abounded, seeds, fruits, nuts, roots and shoots could have made an important contribution to the diet. Pike inhabited the river, where roach, rudd, perch, bleak and sticklebacks would also have been found. Dolphins may have swum upstream and been stranded on gravel banks, while the presence in still waters of the European pond tortoise suggests a climate slightly warmer than today. Birds that are known to have existed include the eagle owl, long extinct in Britain, shoveller duck, cormorant and two birds that are now rare and localised, the red-breasted merganser and the capercaillie.

Although the fossil environmental evidence allows us to reconstruct this fairly detailed picture of the early stages of human life in Britain, our knowledge of man is limited to the clues provided by the Swanscombe skull fragment, the carefully made handaxes and associated prey remains. Folk may have lived in small migratory groups and as yet there is no information of dwellings or permanent camp sites. Even so, perceptions based on Red Indian hunting life in the north-eastern USA just before the arrival of Europeans may be much more accurate than others based on cartoon cavemen.

As this interglacial era drew to its close the climate chilled and Norway lemmings appeared; other sub-arctic fauna colonised the land as the temperate wildlife retreated to warmer climes and the pond tortoises froze to death. England then became the abode of the woolly mammoth, the woolly rhino, the reindeer and the bison, with the spotted hyena and the glutton or wolverine being amongst the less attractive carnivores. Bears, lemmings, snow voles and hamsters were also present and red deer and wild horses persisted. Human hunting bands would have crossed the dry and barren Channel to visit Britain during the milder episodes in the glacial climate and we know that around 225,000 years ago, thus roughly contemporary with the Swanscombe community, early members of the Neanderthal human line periodically found shelter in a cave at Pontnewydd in Clwyd.

An interglacial and another severe glaciation intervened before the retreat of the ice and the dawning, around 10,000–12,000 years ago, of the interglacial which has seen the flowering of human civilisation. A new ice age may, on the geological scale, be just moments away. It would certainly involve an extinction of industrial civilisation and a time of great cleansing for our planet.

Mammoths depicted in the frigid Norfolk landscape of around 20,000 years ago by N. Arber. Norfolk Museums Service.

Although the tangible evidence for their presence is modest, Neanderthal hunting bands certainly visited Britain in the last interglacial, running from about 125,000 to 70,000 BC. The variable climate of this period ranged from cool to relatively warm and mammoth, horse, hippo, deer, bison, ox, lion, wolf and rhino were all included amongst the British wildlife. The Neanderthalers, whose brains were often larger than those of modern folk, were exceptionally muscular, perhaps adapted to physically demanding foraging expeditions. Figure 4 depicts a Neanderthal band at a cave-mouth shelter with different members engaged in using firesticks, cleaning a hide with a flint scraper and shaping stone handaxes.

After the last glaciation they were totally eclipsed by humans of the Cro Magnon type who very closely resembled ourselves. Evidence from the Middle East shows a Neanderthal belief in the afterlife, but the earliest British evidence of such a belief comes from Paviland Cave in the Gower peninsula. Here around 15,000 or perhaps 30,000 years ago a lightly built Cro Magnon youth was buried in a cave-floor grave. He wore a necklace of wolf and reindeer teeth and was provided with grave goods in the form of

A reconstruction of a cave settlement of Neanderthal hunters of around 70,000 years ago by Giovanni Casselli. By permission of the National Museum of Wales.

*The burial of the 'Red Lady',
actually a young man in
Paviland Cave, Gower,
reconstructed by Giovanni
Caselli. By permission of the
National Museum of Wales.*

shells, rods of ivory, a bracelet and the skull of a mammoth. During the funeral ceremony red ochre was strewn on the corpse, perhaps to restore a living complexion. Human life was now firmly established in this appendage of Europe.

At Home in the Forest

THE GLACIAL ERA WITNESSED COUNTLESS comings and goings. As the climate eased, so herds of deer and horses with their human predators in tow would recolonise the wilderness of England. But as the glaciers and ice sheets advanced again the landscape would no longer resemble Sweden but come to look like Greenland. Eventually, and with at least one sudden relapse, the climate shifted from being sub-arctic and became locked into a temperate regime. Over a period of perhaps half a million years communities in Europe had perfected a culture that was finely attuned to hunting the vast migrating herds of herbivores across the open tundra plains. The finest flowering of this culture is preserved in the cave paintings at sites like Lascaux, Arcy sur Cure, Rouffignac, Pech Merle and Font de Gaume, all in France, where the beasts of the chase seem to have been portrayed as part of a ritual which would bring success to their hunters. Here we can see the stocky wild horses – some brown, some black, some dappled, defiant bison, red deer, woolly rhino, aurochs and mammoth. (It is interesting that horses painted on cave walls in the Basque provinces have striped markings on their shoulders and legs and that such faint markings were discerned on Devonshire dun ponies by Charles Darwin.)

One might imagine that the warming of the climate would have been welcomed by the hunting groups of the Old Stone Age, but in fact it must have produced a crisis which deepened as generation succeeded generation. Departing with the cold went the great herds which grazed the open tundra. No longer could one climb a naked, wind-blasted hilltop and spy out the distant, slowly moving masses of horses, deer and oxen. The land was becoming cloaked in trees and, in the shelter of the woodland, creatures were fewer and more furtive. Group efforts which might have slain a whole herd of panic-stricken mammoths might now have been expended and not even have succeeded in the capture of a single flighty stag. There is also something mysterious about the disappearance of large animals which had survived several episodes of glaciation and warming and countless millennia of human predation. The giant deer, straight-tusked elephant, rhino and woolly rhino, cave bear, hyena, musk ox, mammoth and a former species of bison all disappeared – and experts just do not know why. Could they not survive without the tundra grazings; was the final cold stage of the last glaciation unbearably severe; or did man hunt his prey to extinction?

In time a lifestyle evolved which was adjusted to harvesting every possible food source from the wood, swamp, lake and seashore. The great hunt and the winter cold store were replaced by a swift succession of minor successes in hunting and gathering within a life which was finely tuned to the changing of the seasons and the garnering of every little incentive that Nature offered. This was now the 'Mesolithic' period or Middle Stone Age, a fascinating era sandwiched between the heroic epoch of the Ice Age hunter and the dawn of peasant farming.

Today the Vale of Pickering in Yorkshire is a flat and unspectacular agricultural interlude which intervenes between the scenic splendours of the North York Moors and the chalk sea cliffs of the Yorkshire Wolds. Once it held a vast lake of glacial meltwater and before the lakes in the Vale silted and withered away a site at Star Carr was occupied which was destined to preserve the most illuminating evidence of Mesolithic life. According to the radio-carbon clock, Star Carr was occupied around 7500 b.c. but in real years the true date might be more than 1000 years earlier. At this time, and for about 1500 years after, Britain was still an appendage of Europe, linked to the continent by a low marshy landbridge which had its flanks in Yorkshire and Kent. So settlers could wander here from homelands in the area of modern Denmark, Holland, Belgium and Northern France.

Arriving at Star Carr in the warm Mesolithic summer we find the site deserted, for in this season the community fragments and migrates. And so we are free and safe to potter and pry amongst the debris of their winter occupation. The camp site lies beside a lagoon of the shrinking lake and covers about 300 square yards (250 m²). Reed swamp fills a zone at the junction of the lake and the land and willows grow in the damp gravels at the lakeside. Although the climate has become milder in winter and warm in summer the hardy pioneering shrubs and trees have not yet yielded to temperate woodland. Birch forest and stands of pine blanket the country-side, although hazel, which is resistant to both natural and man-made forest fires, is expanding. Elm, oak and alder are becoming established and will soon displace the pines and much of the birch.

Birch trees have been felled with stone axes and dragged to the lakeshore to build a platform of timber and brushwood in the reedswamp, while stones, clay and moss have been spread over this platform to form a living area upon which flimsy tents are pitched. The campsite is littered with discarded tools and the bones of prey, so that by making a careful

inspection of the debris we can learn a good deal about the hunting life. The red deer clearly appears to have been the main prey animal, followed in importance by the roe deer and the elk; the aurochs and the pig were also frequently hunted. The Star Carr hunters were also prepared to pursue smaller and perhaps less palatable game, as the opportunity arose, for the bone debris also includes the remains of the beaver, badger, fox, marten, hare, hedgehog, pintail duck, lapwing and grebe. One skull found amongst the litter provides us with the earliest known evidence for the domestication of animals in Britain; it belonged to a dog which was not too many generations removed from its wolf forebears. Though doubtless providing loyalty and companionship to human masters which it regarded as pack leaders, the dog would have proved useful as a tracker and pursuer of wounded game. There is some evidence that the campsite is not completely deserted during the summer months, for we also find relics of summer visiting birds, the crane and the white stork, while some of the roe deer skulls have their summer antlers attached. Given the lakeside setting and the frequency with which other such sites have produced evidence of fishing it is a little surprising that bones of pike, eel and salmon are lacking. Perhaps a constriction and rapids on the river Derwent downstream, have prevented the fish from reaching our lake.

Although it is easy to detect the different contributions to the hunting

The Mesolithic camp site at Star Carr as visualised by Alan Sorrell. The Illustrated London News Picture Library.

15

Generalised reconstruction of a Mesolithic hunter-gatherer-fisher camp by Timothy Taylor based on information from several excavated sites.

diet it is harder to gauge the importance of vegetable foods. The age of farming still lies a few thousand years in the future but the woods abound in edible fungi, roots and shoots. Many of the discarded tools might as easily have been used for scraping and grating roots and tubers as for cleaning skins or barbing weapons. Confirmation that vegetable foods are also sought is found in the form of an elk antler which has been fixed to a wooden shaft to create a mattock that is useful for grubbing up roots – and we can be sure that the bountiful hazelnut harvest is not overlooked.

Flint, the by-products of hunting and the resources of the forest are all worked to create a sophisticated, versatile and varied tool kit for human survival. Large flints are chipped to produce the axes and adzes used for digging and felling while flakes split off the flints provide razor-sharp scrapers for slicing meat and cleaning hides. Minute triangular fragments of flint are skilfully created by rapping flint flakes with a bone or antler baton and these 'microliths' are used to edge, point and barb weapons. From the discarded items we can see that birch resin is used to glue the microliths to their shafts. Sharpened flints are also used as awls for piercing hides and as tools for gouging out long slivers of bone or antler. These are then skilfully notched along one side to create long, many-barbed heads for spears and harpoons.

Not only do animals furnish the weapons for slaying more animals, they also yield skins and leather for clothing, bedding, tents and bindings, sinews for thread, tallow for lamps, pins or toggles of elk bone for fastening garments, and drinking horns. The occupants of Star Carr being absent, we cannot know whether their tailored costumes of leather and fur are richly decorated, fringed or embellished with animal whiskers, teeth or claws, but we do discover that they wore beads of shale and amber (fossilised resin) which can be collected on the North Sea beaches. In addition, fragments of iron pyrites were sought, not for ornaments but to serve as strike-a-lights for starting fires. The most intriguing items amongst the household debris are the numerous stag 'frontlets', portions of red-deer skull with antlers attached. The frontlets are made lighter by paring and shaving away the bone and it is clear that they serve as stag head-dresses. Possibly these are worn during clan rituals but a more practical use is probable – for we know that some North American Indians used similar headgear as disguises when hunting deer.

The campsites would seem to have accommodated several family groups with a total population of around two dozen men, women and children. At this time of the year the community is dispersed in upland and coastal hunting and gathering groups. The seashore is just about eight miles or a

A Mesolithic hunting and fishing settlement of around 7000 BC as reconstructed by Giovanni Caselli. By permission of the National Museum of Wales.

two-hour walk away and the lofty hunting grounds of the North York Moors are equally accessible. Given the vast accumulated experience which the folk have inherited, survival during the seasons of plenty poses few challenges, while in the winter the fragmented bands re-combine in lowland settings like Star Carr. This is the season for socialising and ritual, for storytelling and for passing on the experiences of the chase. During the season of togetherness marriages can be made while proven leaders can pass on their knowledge of the whereabouts of herds, honey, nuts and other life-saving resources to the youngbloods of the clan. If the lessons are well taught then the clan elders can be supported and sustained when they are too old for the hardships and exertions of the hunt.

The red deer was the mainstay of life at Star Carr and in winter and spring the herds foraged in the shelter of the nearby woods, divided into groups of stags and groups of hinds and youngsters. Bands of hunters would rise early while the embers of their camp fires were still smouldering. The concentrated groups of stags formed attractive quarry and although the hunters lacked the speed to catch their prey or the weapons to kill a full-grown stag outright the dice were still loaded in their favour. Individual animals could be stalked, wounded with arrows or bone-tipped spears and then relentlessly pursued until exhaustion and the loss of blood allowed the animal to be caught and despatched. Groups of animals could be driven into snowdrifts, frozen lakes or marshes and slain *en masse*. Only the strongest of the strong could carry a red deer carcass for any distance

Red deer stags fighting. The red deer was the favoured prey of many Mesolithic hunting groups. Richard Muir.

and the animals were butchered at the killing site with only the best joints and haunches being taken back to the encampment. The red deer remains at Star Carr are of stags with their full-grown winter and spring headgear; the antlers are shed in April.

In the spring the herds would move from the sheltered valleys to the upland browsing and grazing sites and the hunting communities would similarly disperse, some families probably following the deer and also hunting aurochs and boars with bows and arrows, others fishing and seeking shellfish and stranded whales along the seashore. The majority of the hunters probably occupied small summer campsites standing in lofty situations on the North York Moors at the junction of the treeline and the open heath. Following in their footsteps we would find the flint and branch debris of arrow-making scattered around the embers of the camp fires. While venison is luxury fare today the coming of summer would have allowed hunters to vary their diets as roots, shoots and then nutritious fruits and nuts became available. With the game ranging freely in the summer months the hunters may have found it worthwhile to burn back the woodland which was colonising the high plateaux, thus creating attractive open pastures and hunting grounds as well as flushing out the game which sheltered amongst the shimmering birches. Gradually hunting may have given way to herding, while captive deer could have been fed on ivy to ensure a secure emergency reserve of winter rations.

The folk of Star Carr had a way of life which was finely adjusted to the hunting and gathering resources of their environment. Their success as hunters may sometimes have led to a needless overkilling of game and there could have been scope for progress in the direction of the herding and culling rather than the hunting of deer. We know that the full domestication of animals was achieved on the Channel shores of Europe and that the Mesolithic peoples of both Brittany and Cornwall gained the seamanship needed to engage in deep-sea fishing for hake, mackerel, cod and saithe. Even so, it is difficult to imagine that they could have advanced much further towards civilisation. The next step forward required a revolution. Eventually this would arrive in the form of settled farming.

CHAPTER THREE

Temples in a Shrinking Forest

MOST ACCOUNTS OF PREHISTORY PRESUME that farming was brought to Britain by waves of seaborne immigrants from the continent. It is no less possible that the introduction and establishment of farming, beginning some time around 5000 BC, was achieved by gentle conversion rather than by traumatic invasion. The adoption of settled agriculture on the margins of the continent cannot have escaped the notice of the deep-sea fishermen of southern England, and these same people had the boats needed to import the seed grains, sheep and cattle necessary to secure footholds of farming in England.

Most of the products of farming had diffused across continental Europe as agriculture expanded from its homelands in the Middle East. In this way Britain adopted the domesticated cattle, sheep, goats and pigs and cultivated strains of emmer wheat and naked barley. The innovations spread across the British Isles quite rapidly, so that a way of life rooted in mixed farming rather than hunting was established at remote Ballynagilly in Co. Tyrone by about 4500 BC. Here the countryfolk lived in squarish plank-built farmsteads which were scattered around the farmlands rather than being clustered in villages. As the farming life gathered new converts from the hunting communities so the pressures on the land increased and often soils became overworked and barren. Scrub advanced across the established ploughlands, new clearings were hacked from the forest and grazing animals browsed the scrub, nipped off the spreading seedlings and so assisted the establishment of pastures. At Ballynagilly a way of life which was centred on raising livestock rather than on mixed farming had developed by about 3700 BC.

The initial stages of farming had involved the hacking-out of clearings in the virgin wildwood, though in many places the burning of woodland by Mesolithic hunters had already created inviting expanses of open country. The native forest included all the familiar deciduous species of the modern countryside, with the exception of ornamental species, such as the horse chestnut and sycamore, which were introduced in relatively recent times.

The wildwood contained a mixture of familiar deciduous trees of all sizes and ages, though beech was absent or localised and confined to the southern counties. Throughout the Midlands, East Anglia and the south the small-leafed lime was the dominant tree while oak and hazel woodland had ascendancy from the Trent to the Scottish Highlands and over much of Wales. In the Highlands the birch and pine forest, which had characterised the English countryside in early Mesolithic times, still held sway and would endure in many parts until medieval or later times. In the south-western extremities of England and Wales hazel, oak and elm were the commonest trees. As the farming life took root the elm diminished throughout England. The insect (*Scolytus scolytus*) which carries Dutch elm disease was present at this time, although the clearance of stands of elm to create farmland and the stripping of elm leaves for fodder could also have caused the decline. Once felled, trees were burned and their ashes provided a potent fertiliser, but the days of pioneering farming were quite swiftly succeeded by the establishment of a much more organised field-scape. The discovery of ancient fieldwalls buried beneath beds of peat at several sites in Co. Mayo shows that before 3000 BC vast tracts of countryside hereabouts were divided into geometrical patterns of small rectangular fields bounded by drystone walls. This type of Stone Age landscape must have resembled fieldscapes of walled enclosures which exist today in many parts of England and Wales.

As farming expanded and the wildwood islands contracted, so the competition for land and the threats of organised warfare increased. Some communities were forged as people gathered together to seek security and capitals were created as chieftains imposed their domination over neighbouring territories. One of the most intriguing centres of power and defence was at Carn Brea, in Cornwall.

Few landmarks indeed are as redolent of history. The granite hill of Carn Brea towers between the modern industrial towns of Camborne and Redruth. Three peaks overlook the summit ridge, two of them encircled by the ramparts of an Iron Age hillfort, its interior displaying the relics of more than a dozen circular Iron Age dwellings. On the eastern peak the remains of a small medieval castle and chapel were repaired in the 1770s to serve as a status symbol for a local tin and copper mining dynasty, enlarged about a century later to accommodate tenants and a beacon for shipping and then further enlarged in 1979 to include a restaurant. The central peak culminates in a 90-foot (27-m) granite monolith erected in 1836 to commemorate a prominent local nobleman, tin baron and freemason, Lord de Dunstanville and Basset. This monument has been described as a 'slightly glorified chimney stack' and if it does not enhance the natural scenery at least it echoes the derelict chimneys of the tin mines which punctuate the countryside below.

Masked by heather and bracken are the remains of fortifications which

are more than twice as old as those of the Iron Age hillfort and excavations
undertaken in the 1970s provide insights into the Neolithic phases of
human life on Carn Brea. The first settlements on the commanding hill
were undefended, but around 3700 BC a defensive wall of massive granite
boulders was built around the eastern summit, linking up a number of
craggy outcrops and thus creating credible defences for the community
within. The great wall stands about 6.5 feet (2 m) tall and encloses a hilltop
area of well over 8000 square yards (7000 m²). To build it a labour force of
thirty men would have had to work for about four months, toiling for ten
hours each day.

Were we able to visit the settlement in its Neolithic heyday we would see
that the flanks of the hill below the boulder wall are cultivated, while just
outside the wall are patches of blackened stone and earth from hearths of
campfires where people cook and gather at dusk. In one place the wall is
fronted by a ditch just over 3 ft (1 m) deep where smelly household rubbish
is gradually accumulating. Stones from the cultivation plots have been

cleared and gathered in piles or 'clearance cairns'. Wheat is the main crop and it is ground into flour on saddle-shaped quern stones. The walled village and its agricultural fringe are protected by another circuit of fortifications breached by defended gateways.

Inside the wall the surface of the summit has been modified to create eleven level platforms which support the various dwellings of a village of 150 to 200 inhabitants. We can explore one of the homes which is built as a lean-to against the boulder rampart. It measures about 8 ft by 22 ft (2.5 by 7 m), one long wall being formed by the rampart and the other consisting of a woven hurdle-like structure supported by upright posts. The doorway lies at the southern end of the dwelling and the entrance is occupied by a hollow in the floor used as a working area. Inside there is a hearth which is situated beside a second working hollow. A series of pits aligned along the main axis of the house are used for storage and some of them hold pots. The age of the potter is still in its infancy and these crude, plain, hand-made vessels still mimic the appearance of the leather bags which were previously used for storage. The bag-shaped pots have projecting lugs which serve as handles and some of the lugs are perforated, allowing these pots to be hung on thongs. Since the floor surface is rather uneven, the rounded bases of the vessels can be pressed into the earth to stand upright in places where a flat-bottomed vessel would topple over.

The villagers of Carn Brea were certainly not introspective and had trading contacts which extended far beyond their own dominions. A nearby quarry was worked to produce greenstone used for axe-making, the axes being roughly shaped at the quarry and then taken to Carn Brea for grinding and polishing. The finished axes were then traded overland with communities living as far away as Wiltshire. The return trade brought flint from Dorset and Wiltshire which could be shaped into arrowheads and scrapers. At the same time that the village was developing its important axe-exporting industry it was heavily engaged in importing its pottery from a 'factory' situated in St Keverne parish in the Lizard Peninsula some 17 miles (27 km) away. Already industries and trading networks involving the necessities of farming life – axes for felling and hoeing and pots for storing produce – had been established.

The Carn Brea fortified village was not unique in Cornwall. Other granite outcrops, like Helman Tor, also supported defended hilltop villages, while farmsteads and hamlets were scattered across the moor and lower lands into which the farming communities were expanding their operations. Each of the hilltop village communities must have dominated the affairs of the smaller neighbouring settlements while commanding the commerce and trade routes of their regions. As free and fertile lands became scarcer and population greater, so jealousies and rivalries flared into wars. Around 3400 BC a section of the rampart wall collapsed, crushing a bowl and entombing a mass of charcoal. It was never rebuilt. Archaeologists excavating at Carn Brea have discovered almost a thousand leaf-shaped flint arrowheads scattered across the village site. Most probably they result from a successful siege and invasion of the village by members of a rival farming tribe.

Very little is known about the religious life of Carn Brea, but as the period progressed a fervour developed in Britain which culminated in the development of the new and now world-famous religious foci at Avebury and Stonehenge and the creation of a host of monumental tombs and lesser temples. Much has been written about the Avebury complex of ancient monuments, but if we are to appreciate them as living centres of ritual and belief then we must be able to picture them standing within the countrysides which existed at the times of their creation. At the dawn of the age of farming the locality was covered with broad-leafed forest within which the hunting peoples had created a number of clearings. When farming arrived it did not displace the hunting traditions. The conversion seems to have been gradual and those who farmed also continued to hunt the aurochs, red deer, roe deer and wild boar and to gather crab apples, sloes and hazelnuts. Grain crops were sown in the existing valley clearings and areas

The stage by stage exploitation of the countryside around Avebury, showing the progressive removal of the woodland, and the expansion of open countryside and tillage. R.W. Smith/The Prehistoric Society.

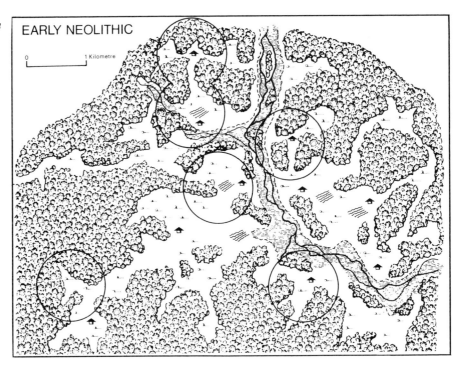

EARLY NEOLITHIC

0   1 Kilometre

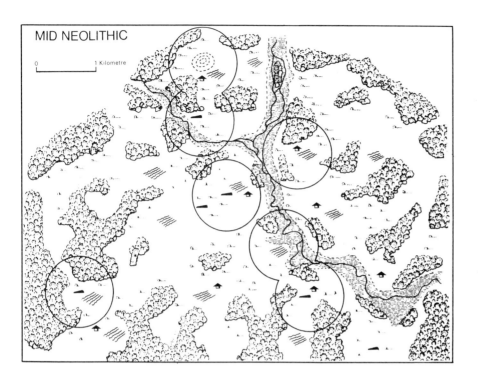

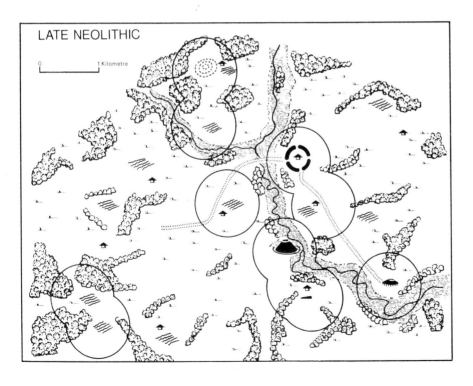

Avebury in its Neolithic form by Alan Sorrell. A concentric ring should be shown inside the uppermost circle. English Heritage.

of woodland were felled, so that fingers of cleared ground ran outwards from the valleys. On some of the farmlands mixed farming was practised while cattle browsed in the woods. However, the ploughing exposed the soil to infestation by weeds. Most weeds of cultivation could be kept in check by weeding and hoeing but one very troublesome weed, bracken, which is poisonous to cattle, sheep and horses, began to spread. The picture which emerges is of a diverse environment, a mosaic of woodland thorn scrub growing in abandoned fields, pastures and patches of plough-land with farmsteads dispersed around the cleared valley corridors.

It is easy to imagine that the countryside was peopled by free, independent farming families whose members could still savour the pleasures of the pioneering life. However, around 3350 BC organised gangs of labourers began digging on Windmill Hill, just over a mile to the north-west of the present Avebury village. The hill existed as marginal farmland with scrub dotting the pasture and with some of the ground being prepared for grain cultivation. It now became the site of massive construc-tional works sufficient to engage a gang of diggers that was 100 strong for around six months.

But were we able to ramble across the completed site we would still be unable to fathom just what had been built and why. The gentle swell of hill top is ringed by three concentric sets of oval ditches; the outermost ditch embraces an area of 20 acres (8.5 ha) and had a diameter of 1200 feet (365 m). The flat-bottomed ditches are not continuous but are frequently breached by causeways and earth dug from the ditches is tossed inward to form embankments. The outer ditch is 16 feet (5 m) wide and 8 feet (2.4 m) deep and the earth and chalk rubble excavated from the ditch have buried the traces of a former farmstead.

Peering into the ditches we see some of the most ghastly sights imaginable, for they seem to have been used as places for the ritual interment of human and animal remains. Some of the bodies, like those of two infants and a dwarf, have been buried intact. Others have been placed in the ditches as dry and disarticulated skeletons, having previously been left to decompose elsewhere, perhaps on funerary scaffolds like those used by some Red Indian tribes. At least the nauseous mass of bones and corpses can tell us a good deal about contemporary life. The people are a little shorter than today, adults ranging between 5 foot 2 inches and 5 foot 11 inches (157 to 180 cm) in height. Several skeletons display the traces of healed wounds, though arthritis was the commonest affliction and the majority of adults suffered arthritic pains in the back, hands or feet, the consequence of hard farm work in all weather. Toothache was another common, painful and potentially fatal affliction, one which could result from the consumption of food which was contaminated with particles of

An imaginative reconstruction of a seasonal gathering at the great causewayed enclosure on Windmill Hill by David Alexovich. From Stonehenge: The Indo-European Heritage *by L. Stover & B. Kraig (Nelson-Hall, 1978).*

grit. The high level of infant mortality reduces the average life expectancy to about thirty years, although the farming communities do contain a number of middle-aged people and just a few elderly folk.

Animals are also accorded ritual burials in the ditches. There are intact skeletons of pigs and goats and the skulls of oxen as well as bones from joints of meat which seem to have been consumed at hilltop feasts. Pottery is also tossed or placed in the ditches, and this can tell us much about the trading contacts of the local people. Pots from the Windmill Hill region include round-bottomed bowls of various shapes but there are also more elegant pots imported from Cornwall and from the Cotswolds as well as heavy decorated bowls of shell-gritted clay with rolled-over rims which are brought from the upper valley of the Thames. The ditches also contain stone querns for grinding grain, the picks made from red-deer antlers which were used in the excavation, stone axes imported from the Lake District, pieces of chalk with cup-like hollows, arrowheads of chert imported from Portland in Dorset and seemingly worthless pebbles from various parts of southern, eastern and western England.

While the ditches seem to have been used as some form of cemetery or, perhaps more accurately, as places where ritual offerings of goods and human and animal remains could be made to the earth spirits, the area enclosed by the ditches also seems to have had a special function. It was probably a great meeting place and trading area serving a role rather like those of the great medieval fairs. Among certain Red Indian tribes the tribal boundaries were disregarded at a certain season of the year, enabling people from far and wide to meet and barter for wares. The Windmill Hill enclosure certainly existed as a great meeting place for many centuries, the ditches being cleared out periodically, to allow for new depositions; meanwhile its very existence told of a society that was organised, capable and able to execute the commands of priests or chieftains.

While the religious and trading centre on Windmill Hill remained in use the countryside below continued to evolve. Felling and grazing reduced the woodland to isolated stands of trees which were set amongst the broad pastures and scattered grain plots. Some pastures were grazed by flocks of sheep, though others were poorly maintained and were being colonised by thorns, hazel and bracken. The advance of the poisonous bracken at the expense of useful farmland was becoming a serious threat and the keeping of pigs, which could root and forage amongst the rhizomes, was the only

A reconstruction of an early farming settlement of around 4000 BC by Giovanni Casselli. By permission of the National Museum of Wales.

practical method of control. Hunting still played a significant role, but now the wild beasts were killed indiscriminately as vermin rather than being treated as an essential resource which should be culled and conserved. Grain growing seems to have been concentrated in a few favoured valley localities which may have been manured and periodically fallowed as sheep pasture. Established pasture was occasionally brought under the plough, but the dense grass and root mat was difficult to work. Often lightly grazed pasture was so dense that the field vole disappeared, being unable to move through the thick herbage and a special plough, the 'rip ard', a curved branch hauled by oxen and tipped with a flint-pointed share, was developed in order to bust up the sod. The pig was increasingly valued and numerous, not only because of its unique ability to deal with bracken infestations but because its large litters of quickly-maturing piglets provided a reliable source of food. Avebury was becoming a major religious complex and the area was obliged to support great armies of construction workers.

Were we able, around 2700 BC, to stand near Avebury at a place that would much later be traversed by the Roman road which survives as the A4 we would see a sight more mystifying and awe-inspiring than the one experienced at Windmill Hill.

A small natural knoll has been encircled by a ring of stakes and hurdles about 65 feet (20 m) in diameter and then covered in turves cut from the nearby pastures in high summer when the winged ants were flying. The turves in turn were covered in layers of flinty clay and gravel and earth to form a cake-shaped mound. This core became the foundations for a radial pattern of retaining walls built of chalk blocks and arranged like the segments and rind of an orange. The compartments were then filled with chalk and rubble quarried from an ever-growing surrounding ditch. This created a gigantic drum of glistening chalk, but then there was a change of plan. A new quarry ditch was opened up and an ascending sequence of five more chalk drums, each smaller than the one beneath, was built to produce a great white hill tiered like a wedding cake. Finally the ditch or moat was extended westwards to obtain chalk to fill the steps of the mound. The product of these toils was the largest man-made mound in Europe, a new hill standing 130 feet (40 m) tall, its base covering 5 1/2 acres (2.2 ha) and its flat summit more than 100 feet (30 m) across.

Could we have been present at the closing stages of the work we might have seen a task force of perhaps 1000 labourers who had been toiling steadily for the last seven years with tools no more sophisticated than wooden shovels, antler picks and wicker baskets. From the quarry ditch the baskets of chalk rubble are passed along the human chain which winds towards the summit. Yet for all its magnificence the Silbury Hill seems to serve no practical purpose and one can still get closer to heaven by ascending the nearby chalk ridge. At least it provides a monument to the productivity of the surrounding countryside, which was sufficient to supply the needs of an army of labourers for many years. The days of the hungry pioneer have been left far behind.

Returning to Silbury Hill shortly after its completion we could ascend to the summit and see some members of a great labour force at work less than a mile away to the north. An immense ditch has been dug which is about 30 feet (9 m) deep and about 70 feet (21 m) wide and which encloses a roughly circular area 1435 feet (427 m) in diameter and 28 acres (11.5 ha) in area. Spoil from the great ditch has been cast outwards to form gigantic encircling banks whose inner faces are stabilised by sloping walls of chalk blocks. Four great causeways, roughly corresponding to the cardinal points of the compass, lead into the sacred enclosure where, invisible from Silbury summit, three great circles of silvery sarsen stone are being erected. Each great sarsen block, the larger stones weighing 40 tonnes, has been hauled here from sites more than a mile (2 to 3 km) away where streams of sarsen fragments, the remnants of a sarsen stone cap which once covered the locality, have accumulated in valleys. Teams of labourers haul on ropes to drag each monstrous rock towards its intended resting place, with swathes of straw being laid on the ground to smooth the passage. The outer sarsen ring follows the rim of the sacred enclosure and is formed of about ninety-eight stones. Two circles are being built inside this ring. Inside the southern circle there will be a central obelisk and a rectangular arrangement of smaller stones, while in the northern circle the design requires an open, box-like arrangement of three enormous sarsens. A ceremonial avenue composed of alternating oblong and diamond-shaped stones sweeps in towards the southern entrance causeway and a second avenue approaches the western entrance. The former avenue runs for one-and-a-half miles (2.5 km) to Overton Hill, the site of a concentric arrangement of stone and post rings, where rituals were enacted before the construction of the Avebury circles and which would be remodelled after their completion. The latter avenue runs westwards for about a mile.

From the creation of the great meeting place at Windmill Hill, around 3300 BC, to the final loss of interest in the great ditched, banked and stone-studded temple at Avebury in the Bronze Age, perhaps around 1600 BC, the locality had a very special significance for the peoples of Wessex. The area was obliged to release armies of peasants to serve as constructional labour on the vast ritual building sites – 200,000 tonnes of chalk were quarried and shifted in making the Avebury ditch alone. Not only was the area expected to release labour for building works, it was also required to support them. We might therefore expect that the countryside surrounding the great monuments would have been intensively cropped. However, this does not seem to have been the case, even though the old forest had been reduced to small and well separated stands of useful and valuable timber. Beyond the Winterbourne stream to the south-west of Avebury there was sheep pasture with patches of cereal cultivation. The Avebury temple was built on impoverished and lightly-grazed grassland where the roots and stems formed a dense mat. Many of the original farmlands had become exhausted and infested with weeds and bracken while land which was cropped for grain and then converted to pasture quite soon acquired a thick sward which could only be broken up for cultivation by ploughing with the specially developed ripard. This was not a virgin countryside, but one in which pigs rooted amongst the bracken and where sheep grazed in pastures that were already traditional features of the landscape.

The modern visitor to the area sees a different and less inviting countryside. Only twenty-seven of the ninety-eight stones in the outer circle of the great temple still stand and the encircling ditch is more than half filled by silts. The hyphenated ditches at the ancient meeting place on Windmill Hill are scarcely noticeable, though Silbury Hill, its turf scarred by the feet of visitors, is still spectacular and a place of mystery. There is just one place where one can see a sight much as it was viewed by ancient eyes. The West Kennet long barrow was built on the skyline of a hilltop just over a mile (2 km) to the south of the Avebury temple. It belongs to the great Neolithic age of temple building and when it was opened in 1859 the remains of five adults and a child were found entombed in the terminal burial chamber. Excavations in 1955–6 explored the side chambers and the two eastern chambers were found to contain the bones of two men, three women, five children and four babies. The two western vaults contained a jumbled mass of bones representing twenty-five individuals. Other bones are thought to have been removed when the tomb was pillaged in the seventeenth century, when Dr Troope of Marlborough took away 'many bushels, of which I made a noble medicine that relieved many of my distressed neighbours'. These were the remains of people who saw Avebury blossom as one of the leading ceremonial centres in Britain; some of them were quite possibly the chieftains or priests who commanded the building works. They were interred in the tomb along with ritual debris of flints, animal bones, beads and pots. Some of the bones may have been brought from the ditches of Windmill Hill, others from mortuary houses and installed in the burial chambers along with the refuse of a funeral feast.

The pottery shows that the tomb stayed in use for around 1000 years. Periodically the great blocking stone at the entrance was rolled back, light would flood into the macabre vaults, the stench of death would seep outwards and more gruesome human remains would be deposited in one of

The interior of the West Kennet tomb. Richard Muir.

the chambers, bones on bones, ancestor on ancestor.

After the excavation of 1955–6 a restoration displayed the great façade of sarsen stones and opened the burial chamber to the public. The bones and smells are gone, the roof is stabilised but otherwise the interior is seen in much the way that it appeared to the funeral corteges around five thousand years ago. One can even see the grooves in one great sarsen which were scoured by the sharpening of flint axes.

33

The Patchwork Countryside of the Bronze Age

LET US SHARE A FLIGHT of fancy. The airliner carrying us on an internal English flight enters a cloud bank at the present moment, but leaves it in the year 1500 BC. As the wafts of cumulus clear from the window we look down on a countryside which looks more unspoilt than outlandish. Networks of hedgerows, ditches and fences hem the little rectangular fields in the patchwork below; small deciduous woods hang to the hillsides; tiny ponds flash in the sun; and in the distance we see the different pastel tones of meadow and heath. Flying at a height of 10,000 ft (3050 m) we cannot discern the details of buildings but we can see the networks of hoof-graven trackways which converge on the hamlets and farmsteads of a well-peopled countryside. Only gradually do we realise that something is amiss, and then not because of what we see but because of what is lacking. There are no dark geometrical expanses of alien conifers, no motor vehicles or bright-surfaced roads to carry them, no suburban sprawls or gaping quarries, no great sulphur-spewing chimneys and, of course, to end our reverie, no airports.

How marvellous it would be if one could sit on a rock and watch the history of a countryside unfold before one's eyes. In a few favoured places meticulous modern archaeological surveys almost make this possible, and in the mind's eye one can see the people come and go and the foundations of countryside being laid. The Shaugh Moor area, overlooking the Plym valley on south-west Dartmoor, is such a place. The area was visited by bands of Mesolithic hunters, who left scatters of flint-working debris around their camp sites and it was cleared of oak forest for farming by Neolithic settlers who would take breaks from farming to go hunting with bows and flint-tipped arrows. During this period of use the countryside became covered with acid grassland which was interrupted by patches of hazel scrub. Oak woods still grew at some distance away and heather was beginning to colonise the highest parts of the moor, although it was still a localised feature of the Dartmoor landscape. Then, for some unknown reason, the pressure of grazing which maintained the grassland was greatly

One of the puzzling stone rows of Dartmoor, this example surviving near Merrivale. Richard Muir.

reduced with the result that woodland, particularly alder woodland, expanded, as did the heather.

During the Bronze Age, in the centuries after 2000 BC, there was a large-scale resettlement of Dartmoor, mainly by pastoral farmers, which produced a new phase of woodland clearance and the expansion of pasture. These centuries witnessed a complete reorganisation of the countryside with the creation of great new field networks and the establishment of scores of new farmsteads and hamlets. Families engaged in resettling Dartmoor around 1750 BC inherited a range of monuments built by earlier communities, and possibly they found them to be almost as puzzling as we do today. These early Bronze Age monuments are cairns, stone rows and stone circles. The cairns are heaps of local boulder rubble ranging from about 10 feet (3 m) to over 65 feet (20 m) in diameter which cover solitary crouched burials placed in 'cists' or boxes built of stone slabs. Some of the cairns are ringed by stone circles and some were created primarily to mark territorial boundaries with twenty-three being built in a prominent chain above the treeline along the watershed of the Plym to mark out the territory controlled by the valley community.

Stone rows are a common, distinctive and mysterious feature of Dartmoor. There are seven of them in the Plym valley, each one built to

35

run downslope from an already existing cairn, with the longest example running for a distance of some 1742 feet (531 m). Elsewhere on the moor are other spectacular examples, like the double stone row on Long Ash Hill near Merrivale or the triple row at Yar Tor, while at Drizzlecombe in the Plym valley there are three rows, one terminating at a 14-ft (4.3-m) menhir or standing stone with cairns and lesser menhirs near by. The stone rows were sometimes built in woodland which had clothed parts of the moor following the reduction in Neolithic grazing; they were in some way associated with particular cairns and they are insufficiently straight to have been used for astronomical observations. Beyond this, their purpose is unknown.

The Bronze Age folk, settling in countrysides of alder wood and heather which were studded with the bizarre monuments of their predecessors, launched a staggering campaign of colonisation and enclosure. Wall banks that are now known as 'reaves' were built, which could run for several miles. From these reaves parallel series of walls divided the countryside into ribbons of territory and cross walls subdivided the ribbons into fields. In the years around 1600 BC the division of land took place on a massive scale and hundreds of square miles of land in different parts of Dartmoor were partitioned. Thus far around 125 miles (201 km) of tumbled reaves have been recognised which enclose about 25,000 acres (10,117 ha) of countryside. The division seems to have involved the establishment of a series of substantial communal territories which were subdivided into landholdings and fields and which had areas of unenclosed common above. Such concerted action could hardly have occurred spontaneously within each community, but must have been part of an organised grand design.

Initially some of the long-distance reaves began as stretches of ditch, bank or woven fencing, the stone walls being built directly upon these older features. Though now toppled and overgrown, it is most likely that the 'walls' closely resembled the stone-faced hedgebanks which are part of the living countryside in most places that border the moor. Fragments of oak, hawthorn and dog rose have been recovered from the reaves, as well as alder, which is not a hedgerow tree and must have grown in some damp pastures. The Bronze Age fields preserve a few traces of cereal growing, which was probably confined to a few favoured localities, and livestock farming was the main activity. Thus in the Bronze Age the broad valleys of Dartmoor did not exist as the wildernesses of heather and bracken moorland that we see today, but displayed countrysides of hedgebanked pastures which rose towards the rough grazings of the open commons.

The most obvious contrasts with the countrysides of agricultural Devon that we now enjoy concerned the dwellings. These were circular, and although they ranged in diameter from 7 feet (2 m) to almost 30 feet (9 m)

A reconstruction of one of the Bronze Age dwellings at Grimspound on Dartmoor. Note the curving passageway at the entrance, which serves as a windbreak. Vana Haggerty/Macdonald & Co.

they were fairly similar in design. The walls of these dwellings were built in the manner of a drystone wall, with inner and outer faces of boulders containing a core of small rubble. The walls were built upwards to a height of around 3 ft (0.9 m) with a gap flanked by large portal stones being left to serve as an entrance. Poles were set in the tops of the walls, each pole sloping inwards to form the rafters of a steep, conical roof which was thatched in heather or straw. The hearth, of fire-blackened stones, lay near the centre of the dwelling and the entrance could be paved or cobbled to reduce the trampling in of mud.

On Holne Moor the building of one new house began with the erection of a circular wall of earth faced in stone around an existing round house built of wattle and daub. Then the old house was dismantled and a roof built over the new one. As a considerable concession to comfort the floor was paved and an inner wall facing of upright planks was constructed. A drainage gully to catch the drips from the thatch was dug around the northern side of the dwelling. While some of the loftier of the solitary dwellings could have served as summer shelters for shepherds, the great frequency of farmsteads suggests that dairy farming rather than the less intensive activity of beef production was the mainstay of the farming economy. The last stage in the occupation of farmsteads on Holne Moor involved the ploughing up of some pasture, apparently using manual labour to haul the plough. Then the land surrendered to peat.

The dwellings could stand solitary or be part of small open or enclosed groupings. As the period progressed some of the open hamlets were enclosed by low boulder walls which surrounded and linked together dwellings. Elsewhere on the moor some of the larger house clusters, like Grimspound on Hameldown, stood in enclosures which had entrances which would allow livestock to be penned close to the dwellings. In the Plym valley, however, the enclosures tended to be small and lacking in entrances. Therefore they could not have been used as pens and must have been entered via stiles. They would have had little or no defensive value but might reflect the dawning of a concept of personal property and the notion of an Englishman's home being his castle.

As the Bronze Age advanced almost all of the tree cover was removed

Characteristic manufactures of the early Bronze Age: a flint dagger, copper axe, barbed and tanged flint arrowheads and ritual beakers. Richard Muir/Saffron Walden Museum.

38

from the Plym valley and the maximum possible number of livestock was supported. The creation of the walled fields allowed grazing to be controlled, while the sheep and cattle were driven down to the lowland fringe in winter where hay would have supplemented the winter grazings. A climate which was on average 1°C to 2°C warmer than today allowed Dartmoor to exist as a vast pasture. Meanwhile, the working of tin, which combined with copper in the manufacture of bronze, helped to support the high level of population in the valley.

In the centuries around 1000 BC the climate gradually deteriorated until a regime similar to or wetter than today prevailed. This caused the waterlogging of the Dartmoor pastures and the leaching out of goodness from the soil. The exhaustion of the land by farming intensified the problem. Peat blanket bog expanded downwards across the grazings and heather and cotton grass replaced the grassland. First the summer grazings were lost and then the walled fields below. Less and less pasture was available and fewer and fewer sheep and cattle could be kept. Coupled, perhaps, with the exhaustion of tin workings, the whole basis of communal life was undermined. One by one the farmsteads and hamlet were abandoned – and by the Iron Age Dartmoor had become a largely desolate heath. Localised attempts to recolonise the moor occurred in Saxon and medieval times. Towards the close of the Middle Ages a very important tin-mining industry flourished and numerous rabbit warrens, some of them operating until fairly recent times, were established.

Even so the moor never regained its Bronze Age dwellings, whose ruins still pattern the moor like fairy rings on a playing field, while masked by heather are the low ridges of earth and rubble which were once the walls or hedgebanks of vast networks of pastures. Entire countrysides of farm-steads, shepherds' huts, enclosures, droveways, pastures and grain plots lie suffocated beneath the peat, monuments to the power of Nature in the affairs of man.

Away from the uplands the impact of the decaying climate was less severe and the greatest challenge may have resulted from the arrival of broken stockmen evicted from the hills and plateaux by the advancing peat. In the valleys and lowlands the vast fieldscapes were also frequently punctuated by hamlets and farmsteads, the most obvious visual differences from the uplands concerning the use of hedgerows and ditches rather than walls and stone hedgebanks, and the use of timber rather than stone in housebuilding. The combination of a contracting resource of farmland with a large and buoyant rural population caused many tensions. These resulted in the construction of fortifications, some grand and some more modest. Society was also becoming increasingly stratified and some of the farmsteads of the late Bronze Age seem to have several features in common with the moated homesteads of the knights and lesser gentry of the Middle Ages.

In the drawing opposite we see a post-excavation reconstruction of an enclosed farmstead built at Springfield Lyons in Essex around 900 BC. The circular buildings with their low timber walls and massive conical roofs of thatch are typical of the period. They stand within an impressive circular defensive enclosure with an outer moat, steep earthbanks, a palisade and walkway and no less than six causewayed entrances. The enclosure is 213 feet (65 m) in diameter and dominates the well-managed surrounding countryside. This is plainly a local power centre and it contrasts with the rustic simplicity of the dwellings which were currently falling into ruin on Dartmoor. Comparable power centres have been discovered at Mucking, also in Essex, and at Thwing in Yorkshire, and they have been described as 'mini-hillforts' and 'prince's strongholds'. The ditch at Springfield was 5 ft (1.5 m) deep and the main entrance was guarded by an elaborate gateway. In the centre of the fortified enclosure the main dwelling had its impressive porchway facing the entrance – and one can imagine the prince or potentate emerging from his home to accept tribute from the elders of the local community or from visiting delegations, or to inspect booty. The excavators of the site discovered clay moulds, thought to have been used for casting bronze swords. Taken as a whole the site epitomises the increasingly hierarchical and militaristic character of life in the Late Bronze Age.

In the Iron Age, following its abandonment, the stronghold apparently acquired a strange religious significance: a sword was ritually twisted and buried at the centre of the enclosure and a horse head in harness was buried near by. Centuries later a pagan Saxon cemetery was established here and some time after the conversion to Christianity, when the cemetery had gone out of use, a late Saxon village developed on its site. Inside the by now ancient Bronze Age stronghold a puzzling building, perhaps with a tower, was built, quite possibly either the hall or the church of a Saxon noble, perpetuating one or other of the former roles of this fascinating place.

While modern archaeological techniques have allowed a detailed under-standing of ancient countrysides, farming and dwellings it is less easy to excavate belief. We know a good deal about funeral practices and can safely assume that life and death, the living world and the spirit world, were regarded as intimate partners. Yet the details of belief remain obscure – burials provide hints of the afterlife but not a theology. About the time that copper working was first practised in Britain, around 2500 BC, the communal chambered tombs, like West Kennet, were sinking slowly into redundancy. The new cult favoured more solitary burials with corpses

being placed crouched in graves or cists along with their treasured
possessions and a decorated clay beaker which held a ritual beverage,
perhaps an alcoholic herbal brew. These graves were often covered by a
cairn or an earthen mound.

After about 1700 BC the concern with burials, grave goods and barrows
tended to wane. Bodies were often cremated and the charred remains were
buried in urns. The barrows retained some of their sanctity for cremation
urns were often buried in the sides of these now venerable mounds.
Throughout much of England the commonest funeral practice between
about 1500 BC and 900 BC involved the placing of cremated remains in
urns which were buried in designated cemeteries located near settlements
or near old barrows. By around 1200 BC this rite was becoming redundant
in many places, after which the whole question of burial and belief
becomes mysterious. Water spirits began to command attention and costly
weapons and metal goods were cast into lakes, rivers, meres and bogs.
Bodies may have been exposed to scavengers or have been deposited in
ditches, marshes and other waterbodies – as is known to have been the case
with criminals or sacrificial victims.

Many Bronze Age barrows have been excavated and modern excavations
reveal the complexity and variability of funeral practices, no two barrows

being exactly the same. Today death is sanitised and one needs a strong stomach to discover how Bronze Age people sent their loved ones to the afterlife. A cemetery of ten round barrows aligned east to west was created at Sproxton near Melton Mowbray in Leicestershire. Here the virgin forest had been cleared by around 4000 BC; the land was cropped and then existed as pasture until about 1750 BC, when the grazings were redesignated as a cemetery. In the case of one of the barrows the first stage of use may have involved the construction of a platform on which the body of a man in his early thirties was allowed to decay. Before the defleshing was complete the body, lying with hands behind back, was covered in a funeral pyre and cremated. The remains were placed in a burial pit and covered in a low mound of turf surrounded by a ring of ten stakes. This stake circle was then superseded by four concentric rings of closely spaced stakes which probably supported hurdles of woven branches. Then the stake rings were burned and a covering mound of earth and stones was built from materials carried into the cemetery site and was surrounded by a low, drystone wall.

About a century after the mound was built a capping of limestone rubble was added, excavated from a ditch dug around the barrow. The cremated remains of several young men and women were placed in pits and sealed beneath the new rubble capping, the burial pits being ritually cleansed with fire before the cremated bones were inserted. The remains of a young woman were accompanied by a broken urn.

It is very easy to envy the apparent rustic simplicity of a period like the Bronze Age, a period when people lacked the ability or inclination to poison their environment and imperil the entire web of life on earth. We can imagine the cowherd strolling through pastures alive with wild orchids, birdsong and butterflies and the shepherd dozing in his summer shelter amidst the thyme-scented upland air. But if we could share their life we would also be obliged to share the ever-lurking threat of famine, accept arthritis as the common accompaniment of adult life, be prepared to act as undertakers when death visited the household and to render tribute to haughty leaders. With the best of the modern world at our disposal it is sad that we are sacrificing the best that the older, simpler world had to offer.

Fighting and Farming in the Iron Age

IN BRITAIN THE IRON AGE began around 650 BC. People were certainly not aware that a new era had dawned, merely conscious that the new metal allowed tough implements to become cheaper and more numerous and weapons to be more fearsome. The changes were most welcome in regions like south-east England which were distant from the sources of copper and tin needed by the bronze smiths. Could we be hurtled back into Iron Age times it might take us a little while to decide whether we had landed into the age of iron or that of bronze. Indeed, many of the characteristics of Iron Age life – competition to secure niches in an overcrowded countryside, insecurity and the highly stratified society – were rooted in the changes set in motion around 1000 BC, or earlier.

When the Romans landed in AD 43 they encountered a society composed of mutually hostile or suspicious tribes, each tribe controlling a territory the size of one or more counties. The Brigantes dominated the north of England with the south-west being the territory of the Dumnonii, Norfolk that of the Iceni, south Wales that of the Silures, north-east Scotland that of the Taezali and so on. In the south-east of England more 'progressive' tribes with stronger continental links, like the Catuvellauni, were recorded. The tribal territories had powerful and treacherous chieftains or kings and some had capitals. Within most territories the land was studded with local power centres, the hillforts, and the preoccupation with defence and security continued at a more localised level to include many of the farmsteads which sheltered behind protective palisades.

Fear and envy had been features of rural life since at least the days of Carn Brea and the other strongholds of Neolithic times. Hillforts were not an invention of Iron Age societies but were founded in the insecurities of the Bronze Age, so that around 1500 BC the prototypes of the hillfort began to be built. However, it was during the Iron Age that these strongholds proliferated and were expanded and improved, so that in some areas, like Wessex or the Welsh Marches, almost every hilltop was girdled in ramparts and ditches.

Croft Ambrey hillfort in Herefordshire and Worcestershire had, like many others, a long period of useful existence during which the defences were enhanced and modified. In the early 1970s an excavation led by S. C. Stanford explored the history of this rather unusual stronghold. The ridge-like hill has the form of an escarpment, with the steep scarp face, which did not require fortification, facing northwards towards Leinthall Common. The first rampart was built early in the Iron Age, around 550 BC, with the fortification of an enclosure of an elongated, rather triangular shape by digging a ditch around the more gently sloping terrain of the dip-slope to the south of the scarp. Earth and rubble from the ditch were dumped in a bank to form a protective enclosure of 5.4 acres (2.2 ha). The fort then became packed with small, rectangular buildings evenly spaced along streets. In complete contrast to the typical circular dwellings of the period, these buildings were rectangular and were supported by their four corner posts. They measured from 8 ft by 6 ft (2.4 m by 1.8 m) to 12 feet (3.6 m) square. Some of them certainly served as granaries not entirely unlike the raised granaries built at eighteenth- and nineteenth-century farms. The other buildings, which were not positively identified as granaries by the discovery of carbonised wheat, certainly seem more similar to Iron Age granaries excavated at other sites than to houses. Other interpretations highlight the neat barrack-like arrangement of the build-ings. Barrack blocks have been associated with Iron Age (and later) strongholds at various places on the continent, though they seem unusual in Iron Age Britain.

Around 390 BC it was decided to enlarge the enclosure and greatly to improve its defences. A new ditch was cut just outside the original defences and the excavated rubble was heaped to form a steep-faced bank towering some 40 feet (12 m) above the ditch and with a timber breastwork running along its crest. The moat-like ditch which fronted the ramparts could not supply all the material needed to build the massive rampart and so a new, broader quarry ditch was opened-up behind the bank. Gateways were provided at each end of the rampart, quite close to its junctions with the scarp face. Each consisted of a passageway around 23 feet (7 m) wide leading to double timber gates.

The entrances to a hillfort were always its most vulnerable points, and in 330 BC it was felt that those at Croft Ambrey should be improved – the decision perhaps coinciding with the decay of the original gate posts. The south-west entrance passage was made narrower and the double gate replaced by a single one. A pair of rectangular guard chambers, walled in local stone, were added to protect the passage and a trench which could hold a timber palisade in times of threat was dug across the entrance. Various other improvements and repairs to the entrances were made in the

A reconstruction drawing of the hillfort of Croft Ambrey as it existed early in the third century BC by A.H.A. Hogg and Dylan Roberts. Hart Davis.

period leading up to 70 BC, by which time the stronghold was almost five centuries old. Finally a bridge was built over the gate passage and a new ditch and rampart were built just outside the main bank.

To the south of the hillfort ramparts was a larger but less strongly-defended enclosure covering 12 acres (4.8 ha) which did not contain buildings but surrounded a peculiar sacred site. This began as a level terrace cut into the slope where, around AD 150, a low mound reveted in drystone walling was built. The hillfort itself was largely abandoned at the time when invading Roman forces arrived in the area in AD 48, but religious ceremonies continued at the mound for about three centuries after the conquest, leaving deposits of charcoal, broken pottery and burned bone as evidence of the rituals.

Despite its excavation Croft Ambrey preserves more secrets than the average hillfort. The neat planning of the enclosed buildings reveals the initiatives of a powerful mastermind, while streets lined by rectangular buildings have been identified at hillforts like Danebury in Hampshire and other hillforts of the Welsh Marches, Credenhill Camp and Midsummer Hill. If, as the excavator of Croft Ambrey and Credenhill argues, the buildings were mainly dwellings then the former fort would have had a population of 500–900, comparable to a substantial village, and the latter might have had one of 4000; it could be compared, in size, to a small county town of today and must have functioned as a regional or tribal capital. The fort on Midsummer Hill was attacked and burned by Roman troops led by Ostorius Scapula in AD 48 and previously contained around 250 buildings. At Danebury round dwellings were built in the outer parts of the fortified area, while in the centre were neat rows of rectangular buildings.

If most of the buildings concerned were dwellings then their occupants must have belonged to a highly organised and disciplined society and one would like to know whether the buildings were conventional homes or barracks housing young warriors. If, on the other hand, most of the buildings were granaries then the hillfort emerges as being more than a bolthole or the prehistoric equivalent of a walled town and appears as some kind of communal bank or treasury. Perhaps the peasants or tribespeople would render surplus grain as tribute to their chieftains. This tribute might then be stored in the communal citadel and be redistributed as largesse. To complicate the question, square buildings which do serve as granaries can be found today amongst the circular dwellings of the Tugen people in western Kenya – but they are also used as store houses and sleeping places for wives and children, and the Tugen have no chieftains.

Without doubt the most famous of all British hillforts is Maiden Castle, subject of the first scientific excavation in Britain led by Sir Mortimer

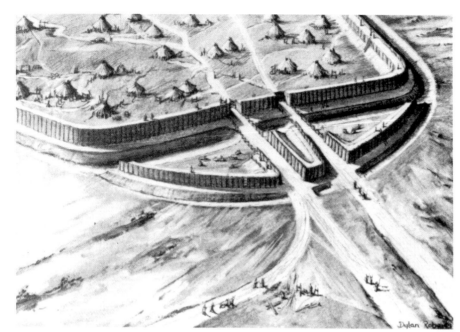

The east gateway of Maiden Castle in its second main phase of development by A.H.A. Hogg and Dylan Roberts. Hart Davis.

(Below) The east gateway of Maiden Castle in its final phase, by A.H.A. Hogg and Dylan Roberts. Hart Davis.

Wheeler in the late 1930s. The fame is understandable, for not only are the concentric tiers of ramparts exceedingly imposing, but also – and unlike many other hillforts – they are quite accessible, the fort rising from level ground a short distance from Dorchester in Dorset. The hill concerned, which has the form of a saddle-shaped, east-to-west ridge, was already a significant ancient monument when the Iron Age ramparts were built. The first notable occupation took place in the fourth millennium BC when a causewayed enclosure, perhaps not unlike the one at Windmill Hill, was built on the eastern knoll of the hill. Two concentric rings of steep, flat-bottomed ditches were dug but this site did not capture the interest of successive generations in the way that Windmill Hill did. However, before the Neolithic period was over a remarkable barrow was built. It ran along the hill for a distance of no less than 1,790 feet (546 m) as a mound 5 ft (1.5 m) high flanked by side ditches and at its eastern end it terminated in a concave arrangement of posts where two small children were buried.

For around three millennia the hill lapsed into apparent obscurity, until 350 BC when a large but simple hillfort consisting of a single rampart and ditch was built. By this time the slumped and overgrown traces of the causewayed enclosure were scarcely visible, although the defences roughly coincided with its outlines. The ditch was 20 feet (6 m) deep, 36 feet (11 m) wide and V-shaped in cross section. About 10 feet (3 m) inwards from the ditch the spoil was heaped into a great rampart which was reveted on both sides by sloping timbers. Entrances were provided to the east and west, the eastern gateway being the more elaborate and consisting of two separate pairs of gates separated by 65 feet (20 m) of ramparts. Flint cobbles were used to pave the area outside these gates, where timber enclosures were built. It is tempting to compare this arrangement with the market square, pens and stalls which so often developed outside the gates of a medieval castle.

After the daunting construction work was completed the defences were neglected, the timbers reveting the face of the rampart decayed and parts of the great bank slumped into the ditch. Around 250 BC, however, all causes for complacency must have vanished and a large labour force scurried to renovate the defences. It was decided to fortify the whole hilltop and enclose an area of 47 acres (19 ha), more than double the original area. A great loop of ramparts extended the fortress westwards and this time the banks were not reinforced with revetments but built as precipitous slopes of rubble descending into the fronting ditch. The old eastern gate was strengthened and guarded by outer earthworks faced in drystone walling reinforced with posts and the new western gateway was also protected by outworks. At the junction of the old and new ramparts a young man was buried in a pit as a sacrificial victim to hallow the enterprise.

48

Again the defences were allowed to deteriorate, until about 150 BC when it was decided that attackers should be kept further from the dwellings sheltering in the interior. Massive new ramparts were built encircling the fort, producing a double set of ramparts and ditches to the north and a treble set facing south. The existing inner rampart was enormously enhanced, towering 50 ft (15 m) above the foot of its fronting ditch. The additional rampart material was quarried from internal ditches and the inner face of the great bank was reveted with blocks of limestone. The double entrances to east and west were enhanced with new outworks, with a Y-shaped ditch restricting the approaches from the east. Within a century a further improvement to the defences was made. The outer ramparts were raised and the entrance defences were made even more elaborate. In the event of assault it was decided that the approaches should be swept clear of attackers by defenders armed with slings. Platforms and guard posts for slingers were provided and thousands of sling stones were gathered from Chesil Beach 8 miles (13 km) away. Excavators discovered a store of some 22,260 sling stones in a pit beside one of the sentry posts. The sentries probably occupied circular dwellings built outside the gateways of the fort in the shelter of the entrance defences.

The dwellings at Maiden Castle were typical of that period. One example had a diameter of twenty feet (6 m). It was built by first digging a series of pits around the house perimeters which were almost 3 ft (30 cm) deep and which held upright posts. Hazel stems were then woven between the posts to produce a strong basketwork frame and a daub of clay, soil, straw, animal hair and crushed chalk mixed with water was plastered on this framework in layers. When the circular wall had reached a height of about 5 ft (1.5 m) its top was strengthened with interwoven hazel rods, a tall post was erected in the centre of the home and rafters sloping upwards at an angle of about 45° were erected to link the wall top to the tip of the centre post, providing the basic framework for a conical roof of thatch bound to a basketwork of hazel rods woven between the rafters. Around one tonne of thatching straw was needed to finish the roof.

While Maiden Castle may have been secure against attack from rival forts or territories it could not exclude the Roman forces. The task of conquering the south-west of England was given to the Second Legion led by Vespasian, a future emperor. Maiden Castle was the key to the conquest of the territory of the Durotriges tribe and in AD 44 the legion, which had bowled over several tribal armies and cracked a number of Wessex hillforts, assaulted the eastern gateway. Thirty-eight defenders, at least eleven of them women, perished here, cut down by swords and catapult bolts, and in the frenzy of the battle the victorious troops hacked at the corpses of the slain. They did not, however, proceed to exterminate the families sheltering in dwellings in the interior of the fort and the survivors emerged to bury their kinsfolk, providing bowls of food and joints of meat to nourish them in the afterlife. The graves were dug through the smouldering ashes of the gateway dwellings. The gateway of the hillfort was slighted but the community was not driven away. They lived within their broken stronghold for around twenty years and then migrated to settle in Durnovaria, Roman Dorchester. More than three centuries later a temple and a dwelling for its priest were built above the silent ramparts, perhaps perpetuating the memory of the spirit god of Maiden Castle.

Throughout most of the country hillforts were the focal points and power centres of Iron Age life, often combining the roles of stronghold, capital and trading centre. Unlike the castles of the Middle Ages they were communal refuges but although they reflect the insecurity of life in a land-hungry society, only a small minority of the population lived permanently in the shelter of their ramparts. There were thousands of undefended or lightly protected hamlets and isolated farmsteads scattered thickly across the countryside. Many dwellings were small and offered only the most basic shelter. But there were others that were well-built and spacious and which might be compared to the manor houses of the Middle Ages.

The interior of the hillfort at Moel-y-Gaer, Clwyd in the fourth century BC as reconstructed by Paul Hughes. Note the contrast between the circular dwellings and the rectangular buildings raised on stilts which have been interpreted as granaries. In the foreground grain is being ground on a stone quern. By permission of the National Museum of Wales.

The reconstructed Pimperne House. Richard Muir.

Such a house existed at Pimperne in Dorset. It was built in a more elaborate manner than the house described at Maiden Castle and two houses occupied the same site successively over a period of four centuries. It had a diameter of 42 ft (12.8 m) and the huge conical roof was supported by an inner and outer ring of posts. The posts of the outer ring were linked together by woven hazel rods which were plastered with daub to form a wall. The entrance was covered in a massive, thatched gabled porch and subsidiary doors stood at either side of the porch and in the opposite wall. The tops of the taller inner post ring carried a circular lintel of beams which supported the rafters. The six rafters were huge elm poles, more than 36 ft (11 m) in length. Their bases were held in slots outside the walls of the house and they each sloped inwards at an angle of 45° and converged at the crown of the roof, some 26 ft (8 m) above the ground, like the ribs in an umbrella. They were carried on the outer wall, and on the lintel of the inner post ring, and were stabilised by a ring beam of lashed posts encircling the upper level of the roof. Subsidiary rafters were then added and purlins of split hazel rods were lashed in place to carry the four tonnes of wheat straw used in the thatch.

The house decayed and tumbled in ancient times but its exact plan was recorded during an archaeological excavation. In 1976 this plan was

51

followed precisely during a reconstruction of the house at the Butser Ancient Farm Project, near Petersfield in Hampshire. From the reconstruction it was found that in addition to the four tonnes of thatching straw the houses consumed rods from eighty coppiced hazels, fifty straight oaks averaging forty years in age and also the great elm poles and ash poles used in the main and subsidiary rafters.

The illustration of a typical Iron Age farmstead at Clay Lane in Northamptonshire's Nene Valley is based on the excavation of a succession of farmsteads which occupied this site. The dwelling, floored with gravel, stood within a ditched and palisaded enclosure and was encircled by a drainage gulley dug to catch the rainwater dripping from its conical roof of thatch. The enclosure was partitioned to provide a separate annexe for livestock and grain was stored in pits dug in the main enclosure. The surrounding countryside was thoroughly exploited, divided into fields and 'estates' with droveways flanked by ditches linking the farmsteads, hamlets and fields.

During the Iron Age the demand for ploughland, pasture and meadow caused further assaults on the woodland. Yet the need for copious, regular and reliable supplies of timber for building, fencing and fuel assured that reserves of woodland had to be preserved and managed. There may well have been scarcely more woodland than exists today, but the typical Iron Age wood was not a neglected wilderness but a productive component of the farming scene. Coppices and hedgerows yielded light timber for wattle

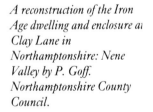

A reconstruction of the Iron Age dwelling and enclosure at Clay Lane in Northamptonshire: Nene Valley by P. Goff. Northamptonshire County Council.

and fuel. Coppices felled on a longer cycle produced strong poles for rafters and the shafts of tools, while oaks, ashes and elms grew tall as 'standards' to prove heavier building timbers.

One of the latest phases in the clearance of woodland occurred in the plain of the River Tees in the north-east of England. Here the countryside was largely wooded until 200 BC. At this time a large pioneer farmstead was built at Thorpe Thewles, near the present town of Stockton-on-Tees. It was built inside a substantial, roughly rectangular enclosure to produce a farming settlement similar to many which existed at this time in other parts of England and not unlike many which can still be seen in East Africa. The house was encircled by a drainage ditch some 62 ft (19 m) in diameter. The posts composing the house walls were set upright in a circular slot and an inner ring of posts helped to support the rafters. The entrance faced south-east, away from the prevailing winds, but there was no massive porch of the type associated with the Pimperne house and other dwellings in Wessex. The enclosure was guarded by an imposing bank and ditch, and while similar defences further south may have been created to protect livestock at night from bandits and rustlers, in this wooded pioneering setting wolves may still have posed a real threat.

The Iron Age settlement at Thorpe Thewles as it existed around 100 BC by Andrew Hutchinson. Cleveland County Council.

53

The farmstead prospered and when the large house had stood for a century or so it was systematically dismantled and several round houses were built inside the compound. Some of these were quite large with diameters of 40 to 46 feet (12–14 m), but most were small, only 26 to 30 feet (8–10 m) in diameter. Some served as dwellings, others as workshops or pens. Some were not built of posts or wattle but of a dried daub-like plaster known as 'cob', with rafters running upwards from the wall top to a tall central post. Most of these buildings experienced two or three rebuildings.

Meanwhile the clearance of the surrounding woodland and the expansion of farming continued rapidly. Grain was grown and ground inside dwellings in stone querns. As the population continued to grow the settlement expanded beyond the confines of the rectangular stockade. The redundant bank was shovelled back into the ditch and new dwellings were built upon and beyond the former defences. The invasion of the Romans, their conquest of southern England and their northward advance did not greatly affect life at this Iron Age village, and throughout the rural north and west an essentially Iron Age lifestyle endured. When the end came, in

The settlement at Thorpe Thewles around AD 100 by Andrew Hutchinson. Cleveland County Council.

the years after AD 100, it was not caused by Roman conquest but probably by the more prosaic problem of water shortage, the nearest source lying in the valley half a mile away. And so after an occupation of around three centuries which had witnessed the growth of a village from the solitary defended farmstead and the creation of open fieldscapes to replace the woodland vistas, the villagers seem to have gravitated to a new settlement closer to the valley water supply.

Because of archaeological work at sites like Maiden Castle, Butser Hill and Thorpe Thewles it is not hard to visualise the Iron Age peoples at war and at work. It is much harder, however, to picture them at prayer. Peoples of the Neolithic period and the earlier part of the Bronze Age left a remarkable legacy of tombs and other religious monuments; the Iron Age people did not. The Roman chroniclers, perhaps over keen to depict their adversaries as barbarian subjects, painted a ghoulish picture of their sacrifices and beliefs. Iron Age religion seems to have involved a remarkable range of gods, some personalised and roughly comparable to Roman deities, some nature gods and spirits of place or of natural features, like lakes or rivers. In the east of Yorkshire groups with strong connections with continental Celts buried their aristocrats under low square barrows along with grave goods which sometimes included dismantled chariots. But in general imposing funeral monuments were not built.

There was a very nasty side to Iron Age religious life, as excavators of a hillfort at Aylesbury discovered in 1987. Portions of at least five human bodies were thrown into a shallow pit. One of the victims was a youngster, buried spreadeagled with a goat to one side and a sheep or goat to the other. Portions of at least thirty animals, many of them lambs, were buried as joints of meat in the centre of the pit and a bonfire had blazed at the eastern end of the hollow. Periodically this stinking mass of sacrificial meat may have been thinly covered with earth. Whatever the nature of the early Iron Age belief concerned, it certainly had some revolting aspects.

While the common burial or cremation rites of the Iron Age are still mysterious there have been numerous discoveries of sacrificial victims. Who were these unfortunate people? Criminals, strangers who had trespassed into a jealously guarded territory, social misfits or, least probably, ordinary members of the community? The most famous victim was 'Pete Marsh', now given the more dignified title of 'Lindow Man', whose well-preserved body was discovered recently in a Cheshire peat bog. He had been poleaxed with a narrow-bladed weapon, then garotted, had his throat cut open and his body was cast into the bog. Different laboratories have offered a conflicting range of dates for this gruesome ritualised murder, ranging from the Bronze Age to the first century AD, though the favoured date is around 300 BC, which lies in the middle of the

Iron Age. He was around thirty years old with a neat reddish moustache and beard (colours perhaps imparted by the peat) and well cut hair, and his last meal was overcooked bread.

Writing in the decades around AD 100 the Roman historian, Tacitus (AD 55–118), described customs amongst the German tribes.

> Adultery in that populous nation is rare in the extreme, and punishment is summary and left to the husband. He shaves off his wife's hair, strips her in the presence of kinsmen, thrusts her from his house and flogs her through the whole village . . . Good morality is more effective in Germany than good laws in some places that we know.

He described how punishment varied to suit the crime: 'The traitor and deserter are hanged on trees, the coward, the shirker and the unnaturally vicious are drowned in miry swamps under a cover of wattled hurdles.' Tacitus also recorded how the spirit of the earth goddess, Nerthus, was drawn around in a cloth-draped carriage pulled by oxen. At the end of the ceremonial visitations the carriage, cloth and goddess were bathed in a secluded lake by slaves, who were drowned in the lake immediately afterwards.

In 1952 the body of a fourteen-year-old girl accompanied by Iron Age pottery was found in a bog at Domlandsmoor in Schleswig Holstein. Her head had been shaved, and she had been blindfolded, weighed down with a boulder and drowned. Tollund Man, discovered in a Jutland bog in 1950, had been choked with leather thongs and Grauballe Man, found in 1952 in another Danish bog, had had his throat cut. All these murders echo the killings described by Tacitus.

He also wrote of the British, some under the Roman yoke, some still unconquered:

> Once they owned obedience to kings; now they are distracted between the warring factions of rival chiefs. Indeed, nothing has helped us more in war with their strongest nations than their inability to co-operate. It is but seldom that two or three states unite to repel a common danger; fighting in detail they are conquered wholesale.

The lack of a vision of one nation caused countless follies and brought the downfall of independence in Iron Age Britain.

Much has been discovered about Iron Age life that is gruesome and frightening – yet we should not lose sight of the fact that the great majority of the people were not strutting chieftains, psychopathic warriors or executioners but unsophisticated countryfolk like the people of Thorpe Thewles.

The Roman Experience

IN AD 43, ALMOST TWO THOUSAND years ago, the Roman legions invaded England and within a few decades most of the country fell under Roman control. In the strictest scholarly circles to call England and Wales a colony of the Roman Empire is not the done thing, because *coloniae* or 'colonies' was the name given to certain of the largest towns which were founded here, like Colchester, Lincoln and Gloucester. Even so, the similarities between the experiences of the British under Roman rule and those of the African and Asiatic peoples who were incorporated into European empires in the nineteenth and twentieth centuries were quite remarkable despite the vast gulf of time which separated them.

In each case the indigenous people had their national identities and political aspirations suppressed and had their more 'barbarous' characteristics exaggerated as a justification for conquest. On the credit side, internal conflicts were quashed and countrysides were policed and pacified, while the economic life of the colonies was greatly invigorated through access to the imperial trading arena – even if the conditions of trading discriminated against the colonial peoples. The similarities go much further: the building of roads to allow the rapid deployment of the occupying troops and then to assist the movement of trade goods; the establishment of planned colonial towns with imposing imperial public buildings; and the intrusion into the countryside of new commercial farms – known as villas in Roman Britain and plantations in the European colonies. We who live in the aftermath of the more recent colonial era should be able to understand the problems faced by indigenous peoples who find themselves propelled into independence with their nationhood still in its infancy.

We tend to look back on the Roman occupation with some pride, seeing it as a great landmark in British progress towards civilisation. The contemporary history of the era is meagre, and all is the work of classical writers who saw the world through imperial eyes. So we can only wonder how the average native peasant regarded the conquest and the domination of Rome. The Roman experience did provide us with our first written descriptions of the British and their homeland. Julius Caesar launched exploratory raids in 55 BC, and in 54 BC wrote that 'The population is immense: homesteads, closely resembling those of Gaul, are met with at every turn, and cattle are very numerous . . . Trees exist of all the varieties which occur in Gaul except the beech and fir.' He was wrong about the beech, which was indigenous in the southern chalklands. Tacitus, the historian of Agricola's campaigns in AD 77–83, provided a brief description of the British with rather unlikely speculations about their various origins. The people varied in appearance, red hair and large limbs apparently being common in Scotland, curly hair and a swarthy complexion in Wales, while people on the seaboard facing France resembled their kinsfolk in Gaul but were more spirited than their subjugated cousins. During the reign of Augustus, Strabo saw some British slaves: 'The men are taller than the Gauls and less fair-haired but looser in texture. Here is proof of their size: at Rome we saw striplings half a foot higher than the tallest men there, but bandy-legged and clumsily built.'

After the conquest, England and Wales were effectively divided into lowland and upland zones. The lowland zone experienced the full forces of civilising influences, the eruption of new towns and villages and the quickening tempo of economic life. In the uplands, native life continued much as before. Civil conflicts and rebellions were suppressed and some minerals, like lead and gold, were quarried. Otherwise the new conditions were evidenced in the main by the periodic patrols from the Roman forts and outposts which ensured that the turbulence of tribal life was kept in check.

Were we able to ramble through the countrysides of Roman Britain we would not see many desolate places, and pioneers would also be hard to find. But, like Caesar, we would certainly be impressed by the numbers of farmsteads, villages and hamlets and by the intensity of the farming operations. The initial colonisation of the landscape had been accomplished long before and Iron Age Britain was already a crowded place; indeed, without the changes and stimuli associated with the Roman occupation, overcrowding might even have caused a collapse of the Iron Age society. Although the Romans seldom transformed the lay-out of fields they did create a greedy new market for farm produce and they also introduced some improved farming techniques, so that a new surge in population growth was sustained.

Some examples of the density of Roman rural settlement have been provided by the archaeologist, Christopher Taylor. The parish of Whittlesford in Cambridgeshire contained five or six Roman settlements, two of which were large, each covering more than 7 acres (3 ha). In Bedfordshire, in both attractive and poor farming areas, settlements were found lying around just 1640 feet (500 m) apart, while in the fertile silt fenlands of south Lincolnshire they were even closer together. Other evidence appeared when archaeological surveys were made along the projected course of the M5 motorway on the eastern side of the Severn estuary: twenty-two Roman rural settlements were discovered on a narrow 60-mile (95-km) stretch of the new routeway. And so we can be sure that were we to be dropped at random into any lowland countryside of England we could look around and expect to see an assortment of farmsteads, hamlets and villages. Only the mountains, the high wet and windswept moors and the most saturated marshlands were desolated or thinly peopled.

Of course, the folk who lived in the farmsteads, hamlets and villages were not Romans but native British people. For them weeks could pass between sightings of a foreigner from any part of the Empire, let alone one of a bona fide Roman from the imperial capital. Many of the settlements were still built in the traditional manner with dwellings exactly resembling those of the Iron Age. But during the occupation not only did they become more numerous, they also became more varied. The native tradition regarded dwellings as circular buildings which could be scattered in a rather haphazard manner around a dwelling site. The Romans, however, were accustomed to rectangular houses arranged in an orderly manner. Gradually the Roman standard was imitated and adopted in many of the native settlements.

Under the Romans a much wider variety of settlements appeared. The towns are well known, while there were scores of places where a resurrected Iron Age peasant family would have felt quite at home. In the uplands the old habits lived on and there were plenty of small villages in the lowlands where the main concessions to change were marked only by the digging of wells and the adoption of coinage. Other small villages relied on manufacturing rather than farming and engaged in producing pots, salt or metal goods. Larger villages developed which displayed much stronger Roman influences evident in more organised lay-outs and rectangular buildings with stone walls, tiled roofs and even glazed windows. Often such villages would have roadside positions and be associated with commercial, administrative or military activities. Small towns also appeared which, though sometimes protected by walls or ramparts, shared more features in common with the larger village than with the prestigious *coloniae* and tribal capitals which were the true towns of Roman Britain.

At Roystone Grange in Derbyshire an agricultural hamlet developed which adopted a few visible Roman influences but which was apparently characterised by its rural rusticity. The archaeologist, Martin Wildgoose, who carried out a study of fieldwalls in the locality, collaborated with artist Simon Manby to produce the drawing of the settlement as it appeared about a century after the Roman landings. The Peak District was occupied and pacified by the legions, the troops then being marched northwards to defend the northern frontier zone where Hadrian's Wall was being built in the 120s. The dry limestone hills of Derbyshire then became integrated into the commercial life of the province, producing wool and lead for the imperial market. British peasants were probably encouraged to work the lead veins which army prospectors had identified and to enclose farmlands near the workings. In this way a combination of mining and farming life was established which would endure into the times of the Industrial Revolution. Land was enclosed with massive drystone walls of a quite distinctive type. They were set in broad, shallow trenches as double rows of large, irregular limestone boulders held upright by small facing stones and with the space between the lines of boulders filled with rubble. The remnants of these 'orthostat' walls can still be seen.

In the reconstruction drawing below we see rectangular thatched and stone-walled farmsteads which contrast with the circular dwellings of the Bronze and Iron Ages. Our view is southwards along a tapering droveway which links upland areas of summer grazings. To the left of the droveway are the small arable fields of the community, while the slopes above the

A reconstruction of the Ramano-British settlement at Roystone Grange in the mid second century AD, by Simon Manby.

farmsteads have been enclosed against grazing to serve as hay meadows producing a store of winter fodder. Despite the simplicity of the scene it was one of many which were largely the creation of Roman rule and contacts. A Roman road had been built within easy walking distance to the north of this hamlet and any peasant free to do so could follow it, join the new network of major roads and proceed eventually to one of the new towns where a grandeur of buildings and splendour of organisation which was almost unimaginable to the Iron Age mind awaited.

Yet in looking at the scene at Roystone Grange I do not sense a deeply distant age – there are too many similarities with the settlement quite near my home at Greenhow Hill. Here, in the years after 1613, lead miners were allowed to build homesteads close to the mines on the Pennines plateau above Pateley Bridge and were provided with allotments of grazing land which they enclosed with drystone walls. I am quite sure that, despite the language barrier, the people living at Roystone Grange in the second to fourth centuries AD had infinitely more in common with the eighteenth- and nineteenth-century miners-cum-smallholders of Greenhow Hill than the Greenhow miners could have with the folk who now occupy the rebuilt and refurbished dwellings on Greenhow Hill. The deepest gulf in history is the one which separates ourselves from our great-grandparents.

Roads and the armies which built them and marched upon them were the means by which most of Britain was brought into and bound into the Roman Empire. Civilisation came with the building of towns. The fully developed Roman town had a number of distinctive features. It had a regular, planned and somewhat standardised lay-out with a grid of straight streets bounding *insulae* or islands of building development which resembled the street-girt blocks in many American towns. It also boasted an array of important and impressive public buildings – the *forum* and *basilica* and baths – and might include an amphitheatre and various temples or shrines. Although the greater towns had much in common they were not stereotyped; differences in their sites, their histories and their individual functions ensured a measure of diversity. The top tier of towns were the truly Roman *coloniae*. These accommodated retired legionaries who were each allocated plots in the new towns. Colchester was the first *colonia* followed by Lincoln and Gloucester, and meanwhile London was expanding as a bustling commercial focus.

Other towns could be established through the promotion of promising existing settlements. At York a civilian settlement which faced the great legionary fortress across the River Ouse was made a *colonia* early in the third century and London became a *municipium* and then a *colonia* just a little before the promotion of York. A *municipium* was a chartered town with a substantial proportion of Roman citizens but which lacked the full status enjoyed by a *colonia*; Verulamium (St Albans) was one of the first to be created. Then there were the *civitas* or tribal capitals established as the Romanised foci of the indigenous territories, which displayed more organisation and planning than the run-of-the-mill small towns and large roadside villages, places like Canterbury, Exeter and Wroxeter.

Our knowledge of the internal lay-out and appearance of the Roman town in Britain varies from case to case, depending upon how later growth has masked the Roman plan and how many opportunities there have been to excavate the Roman levels during modern phases of redevelopment. One of the most thoroughly understood examples is Lincoln or *Lindum colonia*. In the invasion of eastern England the Twentieth Legion established a garrison at Colchester and the Ninth Legion advanced via Cambridge and Godmanchester, skirting the south side of the Fens to Lincoln. Ermine Street was built as a major military highway and a key fortress was subsequently developed upon it at Lincoln.

The town originated in this great fortress built by Legion IX Hispana in the territory of the Coritani tribe around AD 60. The fortress was evacuated about thirty-five years after the Roman invasion and at the end of the first century the site became a *colonia*, founded as a settlement for discharged veterans of the Ninth Legion and of other legions. The fortress was situated in a commanding position at the southern end of a lofty limestone escarpment overlooking the breach cut by the River Witham. The legionary stronghold had turf and timber ramparts, but when it became a *colonia* the new-found civic dignity was expressed by building a 4-ft (1.2-m) thick masonry wall in front of the ramparts and by cladding the gateways in stone. Unfortunately the walls were built without foundations in the ditch which fronted the ramparts, causing it gradually to lean outwards in some places. Within the fortifications was a rectangular area of more than 40 acres (17 ha). The straight main thoroughfare of the fortress, the *via principalis*, ran north to south down the middle of the rectangle on a line roughly corresponding with the surviving street, Bailgate. A second thoroughfare ran between the east and west gates of the fortress, so that the two streets divided the fort into four rectangular quarters. The medieval castle occupies much of the south-western quarter and the cathedral opposite has its west front, nave and great transept in the south-eastern quarter and its angel choir to the east of the Roman ramparts.

In 1978–9 excavations on the site of the Church of St Paul-in-the-Bail discovered the position of the legionary headquarters building, or *principia*, an east-facing timber building which stood in the centre of the fort in the north-western angle of the road intersection. After the evacuation of the fortress the *principia* was demolished and the site was paved. A short-lived complex of public buildings was erected but was succeeded, before the

middle of the second century, by the erection of a new *forum*. This was the hub and market centre of the town. Closely associated with the *forum* was a *basilica*, a large aisled hall running the length of the *forum* which was used for public meetings and law courts and for housing offices used by public officials. In modern Lincoln a length of wall, which stands about 20 ft (6 m) high and is one of the largest pieces of non-military masonry still standing, is known as the Mint Wall. The recent excavations suggest that this is part of the northern wall of the Roman *basilica*. At Lincoln a temple was incorporated into the eastern side of the *forum* and next to it was a well house with an 8-ft (2.4-m) well shaft. In the reconstruction drawing we see the thoroughfare running beside the *forum* and the *basilica* overlooking the

Roman Lincoln by David Vale. The forum occupies the centre and is divided into two parts, the large building of the basilica is to the right and the courtyard to the left is shown containing a temple.
Lincolnshire County Council.

63

market place. A hypothetical temple is shown to the south (right) of the *forum*.

Roman Lincoln had an efficient sewerage system, the main sewer running beneath the north-south thoroughfare and consisting of a stone-walled and slab-roofed tunnel up to 5 ft (1.5 m) high and 4 ft (1.2 m) wide which received the flow from smaller sewers and house drains. Water was brought into the town via an aqueduct over a distance of 2000 yards (1.8 km) from a stream later known as Roaring Meg. The water was carried in 5½in (140 mm) diameter earthenware pipes which were encased in concrete. The pipeline ran underground before being carried on an embankment and then on an aqueduct bridge to the stream. At Roaring Meg water was pumped or raised in buckets to the top of the aqueduct bridge and would then flow under gravity into the town.

A civilian settlement developed on the hillslope to the south of the fortress and continued to expand after the *colonia* was established. Eventually, late in the second century, it was incorporated into the Roman town, being twice as large as the settlement within the walls of the old fortress. The old eastern and western fortifications were extended south-wards by an earthen rampart crowned by a fence or palisade. Then a 5-ft (1.5-m) thick stone wall was built into the outer face of the bank. The north-south thoroughfare ran through the fortified extension to the town, and gateways in the new defences admitted an east-west thoroughfare so that the lay-out of the new town echoed that of the old. At first there would have been some social and administrative distinctions between the proud *colonia* with its populations of distinguished Roman veterans and imposing civic buildings and the new town just below with its mixed immigrant population, but in time the towns began largely to function as one.

Roman Lincoln stood in a region where small towns and large industrial and market villages were mushrooming and flourishing, but it was as different from the rough and ready little boom towns as Dallas is from Deadwood. Like the other great *coloniae* it was a place of status and style, with colonnaded shopping streets, life-size equestrian statues of imperial worthies, metalled roads, an imposing civic centre and great commercial vitality. The main civic buildings were built of locally quarried stone while in the surrounding *insulae* most of the properties were of timber-framing and roofed in clay tiles. Many were arranged around courtyards with shops and booths aligned along the sides of the buildings which faced the bustling streets. Some of the grander town houses were of stone, some with costly mosaic floors or with walls faced in Italian marble. Rustic strangers entering the town through one of its gateways (the Newport Arch of the north gateway is the only surviving Roman archway still in use in Britain) discovered a new world of imperial sophistication and the culture shock

Opposite: *Street scene in Roman Lincoln, by David Vale.*

65

would have left them almost speechless. Indeed, it is doubtful if visitors from places like Roystone Grange had words in their vocabularies which would describe the wonders they had seen.

The splendour of the great Roman towns could not survive in isolation. During the fourth century the security essential to commerce and government was threatened by barbarian raids of a worrying frequency. At several towns walls were strengthened and heightened, gateway fortifications were provided and artillery towers or bastions were added to the walls. Defences which had existed largely to buttress the prestige of a town were now needed for more practical purposes. There was also a decline in interest in urban affairs and a decay of civic pride. Public buildings were allowed to become neglected and a shabbiness became apparent as repair and maintenance work was left undone. Perhaps the burdens of taxes, inflation and refortification sapped the resources and energy of the townspeople.

Although the towns could not exist in isolation and suffered as their communications with the countryside deteriorated, the despondency was less apparent in the rural areas, where expensive, optimistic villa-building

A reconstruction of the Roman farmstead at Clay Lane, Northamptonshire, by P. Goff. Northamptonshire County Council.

projects continued. Like the Roman towns and villages the villas varied greatly. Although they can be loosely compared to those country mansions of the post-medieval centuries which were also the hubs of great agricultural estates they differed in their appearances and in their occupants. Some evolved from rustic farmsteads and others were purpose-built and luxuriously appointed; some stood alone but a few were the foci of sprawling villages; some were the homes of wealthy outsiders and others housed native aristocrats and entrepreneurs; and while some villas echoed Roman lifestyles some may have provided settings for traditional native extended family life.

The contrast between Roman and Iron Age farm buildings can be appreciated by comparing the drawing of the Roman farmstead excavated at Clay Lane, Northamptonshire, with the Iron Age building found there and illustrated in the previous chapter. Less sophisticated than a fully developed villa, the farmstead was a rectangular building measuring about 45 feet by 30 feet (14 m by 9 m) consisting of three rooms set in line and fronted by a verandah. Its walls were of timber set on limestone footings and its roof of a mixture of tiles and thin stone slabs. Sharing the farmstead's walled enclosure was a circular dwelling belonging to a different building tradition and representing a translation of the traditional style of housing into the new fashion for building in stone. In the imperial lands on the continent impressive villas stood as the foci of large estates worked by slave labour. However, the evidence from Northamptonshire shows that while farming became more commercial the traditional rural life was modified rather than transformed by the new conditions and there were still niches for the peasant farmstead.

The villa-owning class was peopled by families from a variety of imperial or native backgrounds, although affluence and a measure of social status were essential prerequisites for entry into the rural elite. Since the villa was both a country mansion and the focus of a commercial farming estate those who invested in such projects sought both security from political unrest and productive farmland with good connections to the urban and military markets for farm produce. Not surprisingly, villas were concentrated in the well-policed and pacified English lowlands where soils were fertile, the climate less moist and turbulent than in the north or west and where roads and markets were well developed. There were, however, some villas situated at the margins of the civil and the military zones of Roman Britain, close to the frontiers of Romanised and traditional life.

One such villa was established in South Glamorgan to the north of the present village of Llantwit Major. This lay in the tribal territory of the Silures, a volatile folk described by Tacitus as being swarthy, curly-haired and resembling the people of Spain. Under the Romans a tribal capital,

Venta Silurum, was established at Caerwent about AD 75 and the Llantwit villa must have served this small but quite sophisticated centre. The villa seems to have developed from humble origins, perhaps from a modest timber villa which was itself preceded by a native settlement. The timber villa may have been rebuilt in stone though a phase of decline followed and it was not until the end of the third century that buildings of style and substance appeared. The villa itself was built to an L-shaped plan with walls of rendered local stone, embellishments in imported Bath stone and a tiled roof. One range contained elegant reception rooms, a dining room and probably a kitchen and shrine, the other sleeping quarters and a bath suite, with a lean-to building at the southern end of the range housing a furnace. Outbuildings surrounded the irregular outer courtyard and were built around AD 300. They comprised accommodation for servants, barns, stables, workshops and housing for estate workers. The two reconstruction drawings portray the villa as seen from the same vantage point. The one by Hughes is based on more recent evidence and contains some differences, with some outbuildings being shown as thatched rather than roofed in sandstone slabs and the site as being unenclosed.

The uncertainties which undermined town life often went unheeded in the countryside. Caerwent was threatened by Irish raiders and around AD 340 a set of bastions to support artillery catapults *(ballistae)* were added to the circuit of walls and the town took on the aspect of a fortress – yet it was at about this time that the nearby villa enjoyed a costly and luxurious refurbishment. Colourful murals were applied to the new plasterwork in several rooms and four mosaic floors were laid. Shortly afterwards, however, the turmoils of the later part of the Roman occupation seem to have reached Llantwit, for evidence of some kind of massacre of men and horses was discovered during excavations. Late in the century the furnace of the semi-derelict villa was used for iron-working, and tradition claims that after the Roman departure from Britain the villa site became the home of Saint Illtud, one of the shadowy figures associated with the perpetuation of Christianity in the Celtic west.

The association between a decaying villa and a forge occurred again at Chilgrove near the Roman Silchester-Chichester road. Here, in an area much closer to the heartlands of the civil zone, two villas lay just a mile apart. Here again the peak of rural prosperity was enjoyed in the first half of the fourth century. Our drawing, by Cedric de la Nougerede, shows one of the Chilgrove villas at this time, with its bath house at the lower end of the range and a new room being added at the upper end. In the second half of the century this villa was burned and abandoned. A forge was built into one of the empty rooms and a gap knocked in one of the walls to give access to carts. Probably the derelict villa was absorbed by its neighbour and used

70

as a workshop for the equipment of its estate. Before the century had ended the surviving villa was also destroyed by fire and the sophisticated commercial life of the villa age disappeared.

One of the grandest villas existed to the west of Hungerford in Wiltshire in what became Littlecote Park, the grounds of a Tudor mansion. A few years after the Roman conquest a circular house of the traditional type was built here and around AD 100 it was replaced by an agricultural barn, an open-sided building with its roof supported on posts arranged like the pillars in the aisle of a church. Bread ovens and corn-drying equipment were installed in the barn. Around eighty years later this was in turn replaced by a flint-walled barn which still endured in about AD 300 when a bath suite was built in one corner. Sixty years later the roof of the barn was removed and its stone tiles were used as the foundations for the flagstones of an open courtyard. The barn was converted into a temple of the old and once again fashionable cult of Orpheus. The temple was associated with a large villa nearby composed of buildings arranged around a rectangular courtyard and entered from a massive twin-towered gateway which was excavated in 1988.

From an anteroom devotees of the cult crossed a courtyard and entered a compact but ornate bath suite with cold, warm and hot rooms and a changing room. Then they entered the sacred area, a rectangular room or 'nave' opening on to a chamber or 'chancel' of clover-leaf shape, both with floors paved in spectacular mosaics. In the main mosaic the figure of Orpheus, who plays the lyre and is accompanied by a dog, is surrounded by figures symbolising birth, youth, maturity and death, represented respectively by Aphrodite, Nemesis, Demeter and Persephone.

Despite the early persecution of Christians the imperial attitude to religion was generally flexible. Foreign deities were assimilated into the broad church of the Empire and one sought not to offend a particular divinity even if one doubted its existence. At Bath hot springs which were held sacred by Iron Age tribesmen were developed as baths and a temple to Sul Minerva, the Roman goddess of wisdom and healing. The Persian god Mithras was perceived as victorious and honest and consequently had a strong following amongst soldiers and merchants in Britain. Local cults, like that of Verbeia, goddess of the River Wharfe, flourished while simple Romanised temples perpetuated the worship of other indigenous gods and goddesses. Christianity appeared in Britain in the second century and in AD 314 three bishops from Britain attended the Council of Arles. The nominal conversion of the Empire to Christianity did not eliminate other competing religions – at Lullingstone villa in Kent a shrine to water nymphs continued in use when the room just above existed as a Christian chapel.

We know more about the appearance of Britain in Roman times than in

Opposite: *the Chilgrove I Roman villa at the height of its prosperity between the early and mid fourth century and partially destroyed by fire in the late fourth century. Drawings by Cedric de la Nougerede. Chichester District Council.*

71

any preceding period. The occupation lasted for more than four centuries and the pace of change was probably as swift as in any previous time. These changes, many of them quite revolutionary, were superimposed upon a landscape which, as we have seen, was already almost fully exploited. There were many differences between and within England and Wales in the early days of the occupation, when the building of roads and fortresses held the limelight; in the middle phase with the growth of towns; and in the later stages, with the gradual decay of urbanisation, the fortification of towns and of the vulnerable coastline but with the continuing optimism in and development of the countryside.

The contraction and collapse of the Empire created problems for Britain which were as acute as any faced by the newly independent states of the twentieth century. Wish and try as they might, the leaders of society were unable to recreate the ebullience and organisation of the Roman heyday. A millennium may have passed before the Roman levels of population were achieved and it took considerably longer to emulate the efficiency of the Roman system of roads.

Opposite: *the reconstruction drawing by Trevor Caley shows a ceremony in the Orphic 'church'. Roman Research Trust.*

CHAPTER SEVEN

The Time of Arthur:
the Darkness that Followed

IMAGINE THAT ANCIENT WRITERS HAVE told of a fabulous city packed with wonders. Archaeologists discover and excavate its site and describe a rather humdrum little town. Who do you believe, the ancients or the modern excavators? I would always favour the archaeological interpretation, but this example highlights the difficulties of understanding what happened in England after the Roman withdrawal. Several contemporary or almost contemporary chroniclers have described the conquest of the country by Anglo-Saxon hordes, yet archaeology argues a different case. The numbers and impact of the invaders are open to question but it would not be easy to exaggerate the depth of the castastrophe which afflicted the country. The culture which emerged from the chaos was not British, Roman or Saxon, while between the retreat of the Empire and the time of King Alfred, a yawning chasm of mystery confronts anyone seeking to recreate the landscapes of the Dark Ages.

In 383 a Roman officer, Magnus Maximus, stripped the Roman garrison in Britain and took the troops to Gaul in an attempt to enforce his bid for the imperial throne. In 410 Alaric's barbarian hordes sacked Rome and it was about this time that Honorius, the Roman Emperor of the West, exhorted the citizens of Britain to look after themselves as best they could. Bereft of any hope of imperial help, assailed by internal breakdown and barbarian raids, the British broke away from the impotent Empire.

What happened next can only be outlined in very general terms. Native leaders attempted to preserve the trappings of Roman civilisation but the severance of the links with Rome and deep, internal divisions gradually resulted in economic decay and political disunity. Commerce was replaced by a lapse into local self-sufficiency; farmlands worn out by centuries of intensive cropping became sterile and broken; and barbarian raiders – Picts from the far north, Scots from Ireland and Angles, Saxons, Jutes and Frisians from the continental seaboard – all harried the margins of England and Wales. The Anglo-Saxons, small numbers of whom had served as mercenaries in the Roman and post-Roman defence forces, settled and intermarried with the British populations and were joined by kinsmen engaged in sporadic waves of immigration.

These events provided the background to the age of Arthur. Many centuries later the legendary Arthur would emerge in France and England as a popular medieval symbol of courtly love and chivalry, since which time his appeal has scarcely waned, so that in the modern age he is a cult figure competing for attention with ley lines and UFOs in the loony realms of 'alternative' archaeology.

Historical information about Arthur is so brief that it can be written on the back of a postcard with plenty of space to spare. In a history of Britain, written perhaps between the late seventh and early ninth century, it is said of events occurring in the early sixth century that: 'In that time the Saxons grew strong in number, and increased in Britain. When Hengest [a

A representation of a Dark Age warrior on a Pictish stone at Aberlemno in Scotland. Note the helmet, round shield, sword worn at the waist and spear held in the manner of a javelin rather than a lance. Arthurian cavalry might have been similarly armed. Richard Muir.

mythical Saxon leader] was dead, Octha, his son, crossed from the north part of Britain to the kingdom of Kent. From him the Kings of Kent spring. Then Arthur fought against him in those days, with the Kings of the Britons, but he was their leader in war.' There follows a list of Arthur's battles, culminating in the twelfth battle 'on Mount Badon, in which there fell in one day 960 men from the onslaught of Arthur alone, and no one laid them low, save he alone.' The Welsh Annals, dating perhaps from the tenth century, record the Battle of Badon in 516, 'in which Arthur carried the cross of our Lord Jesus Christ for three days and three nights on his shoulders, and the Britons were the victors.' The same Annals contains the following entry for 537: 'The Battle of Camlann, in which Arthur and Medrant [Modred] fell.' There is an earlier source than these, Gildas, an embittered monk who blamed the collapse of Roman civilisation here on the corruption of British leaders. Gildas would have been a contemporary of Arthur yet his contemptuous account of the ruination of Britain contains not a mention of him.

Quite possibly Arthur did exist, not as a king but as a commander of forces seeking to preserve a Christian Romanised society from the tides of pagan barbarism. Arthur could have operated in the far north of England or in the west but it is most unlikely that we will ever learn very much more about him. So far as the appearance of the countryside of Arthurian Britain is concerned, there is nothing of substance to be found in any of the literature. Consequently only archaeology can furnish the answers.

We know that the countrysides of Roman Britain were very productively worked – they must have been to support the wealth of population revealed by archaeologists who have identified as many as four rural settlements per square kilometre of land in the most favoured countrysides. Remember too that a century before the Roman conquest and occupation Caesar had discovered an immense population where homesteads were met at every turn. The evidence for settlements in the centuries following the Roman withdrawal is much more modest and seems to tell us of a great catastrophe or sequence of catastrophes. Economic crises, war, instability, environmental decay and plague each had their part to play. Roman countrysides would not have looked drastically different from those areas where the scenery is still unspoiled by the ravages of agri-business. Picture a scene in, say, Devon or Shropshire with small hedged pastures and ploughlands interspersed with useful little woods, and then imagine what would have happened as the agricultural market contracted and population declined. Thistles would spread across neglected pastures, hawthorn seedlings would grow unchecked, woods would gradually expand beyond their confines and entire fields would fall out of use as the farmed area contracted. Events such as these explain how Roman settlement sites are frequently discovered buried beneath woods which were supposed to have been 'primeval'.

Added to the social, political and economic turmoils there seems to have been a marked worsening in the climate. One which was rather warmer and drier than the present climate seems to have given way to a colder phase in the fourth century and then to cold winters and wet summers in the fifth century.

A sequence of events which seem to have been quite typical of the lowland countryside during this period was discovered from excavations at Barton Court Farm in Oxfordshire. Around AD 270 a stone-walled villa was built within a rectangular farmyard which also contained a cottage for servants or farm workers, two wells and a corn drier which may have been used for malting. The villa stood in farmland with little woodland, although oak and hazel were cut for light timber in a coppice. The main crops grown were wheat, barley and flax, with both ploughlands and pastures surrounding the villa. During the fourth century the villa was systematically dismantled but the nearby cottage continued to be lived in until around the time of the Roman withdrawal or a little later, when the occupants moved to a spot near by. During the fifth century a few humble timber dwellings were built close to the site of the former villa and in the sixth century bodies were buried in the old villa and cottage foundations. After the demolition of the villa the farmland continued to be worked but became rather unkempt. Barley and flax were the only crops grown and shrubs began to colonise some of the fields.

Features discovered at Barton Court recur frequently at other sites and seem to form a pattern which illuminates the history of Dark Age England. The deterioration begins early in the fourth century with the decay of urban life and amenities. There was an exodus of wealth from the towns into the villas and the commercial estates which surrounded them. However, the villa boom was short-lived and in the years around 350 the villas were being abandoned, although agriculture of a reduced intensity continued. Farm production was no longer geared to serve commercial markets – which now scarcely existed – but was organised to support local subsistence.

Barbarian raids were not the cause of these ills – a strong and buoyant society could have repelled them. There is certainly no real support for the traditional interpretation that Saxon armies conquered England, exterminating the British and driving the survivors into the western fastnesses. Saxon settlers arrived gradually, settling both in the derelict corners of estates and alongside British communities, sometimes amongst the tumbled walls of decaying villas. The immigrants seem, from the evidence of contemporary cemeteries, to have been quite few in numbers and largely male. Instead of slaughtering the British people they took native wives and their arrival may have helped to reduce the fall in population and abandonment of land. Their effect was largely confined to the southern and eastern lowlands. In the uplands of the north and west traditional British life continued – and there was not the rise in population and conflict which would have been caused if the areas had been inundated by British refugees.

Romans had been impressed by the stature of the Britons, though excavations of cemeteries in Hampshire show an average height for men of only 5 ft 6 in (171.1 cm). By the seventh century this had risen to 5 ft 8 in (175.6 cm), perhaps reflecting the immigration of Saxon men who were larger than the British. Life expectancy in late Roman Britain was only around thirty years.

Most towns were in decline well before the Roman withdrawal. Thereafter occupation of a degraded kind persisted in some places and London may never have been deserted. Frequently strangers would wander through the silent, refuse-strewn streets of crumbling cities. One of the earliest Saxon elegies describes a town which may have been Bath as 'broken by fate, the castles have been decayed; the work of giants is crumbling. Roofs are fallen, ruinous are their turrets, despoiled are the towers with their gates; Frost is on their mortar, broken are the roofs, cut away, fallen undermined by age . . .' With the collapse of commercial life and social organisation the larger settlements withered and rural life focused on the farmstead and hamlet. In the English lowlands these settlements displayed some new architectural features and it has commonly been assumed that their buildings are of types introduced by Saxon settlers from the continent. Even so they do not exactly replicate the rural buildings of the Saxon homelands.

Buildings which resemble 'halls' associated with 'Saxon' settlements have been found at several sites which appear to have been occupied only by the Romano-British natives. At Dunston's Clump, near Babworth in Nottinghamshire, a pair of square ditched enclosures lay beside a cluster of smaller paddocks. Excavation showed that around the time of the Roman conquest a timber building was erected in the southern enclosure, the adjacent area being fenced to create a small yard. In due course the farmstead was rebuilt in a rectangular form with walls of upright posts set in a foundation trench. In the course of the second or third century AD the farmhouse and yard were abandoned, the enclosure containing them still being used in association with livestock farming. A new fence or palisade was erected around the enclosure, which now contained stock pens and compounds, sheds and a larger dwelling: a rectangular farmstead with walls built on a framework of upright posts. The occupants consumed

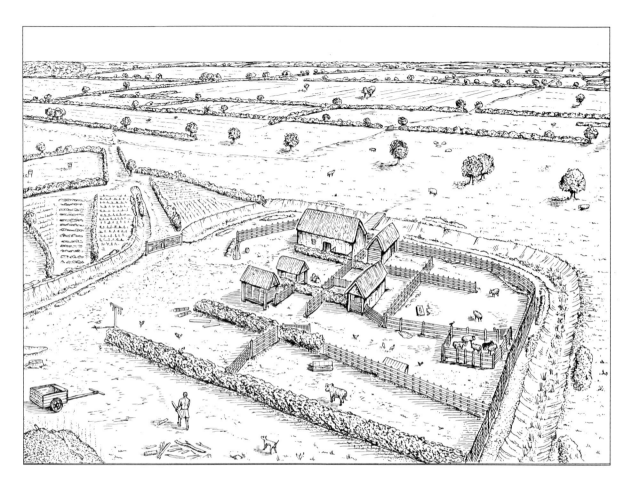

wheat, mutton and pork and the enclosure could have formed the hub of a farm specialising in sheep and appears to have accommodated quite humble farm workers. The area around was systematically divided into fields with a 'brickwork' plan, their boundary ditches forming patterns like that of the mortar in a brick wall. Long parallel ditches with an east-west orientation were cut, with short ditches forming cross-links to complete the division into rectangular fields. Such networks of brickwork pattern fields were quite common and are thought to show a Romano-British organisation of the countryside, though comparable field systems were set out at various prehistoric periods. These particular fields could reflect a development of the commercial farming resources by entrepreneurs from Roman towns, with the day-to-day operation of farming being entrusted to local peasant farmers, like the ones established at Dunston's Clump.

Native timber buildings influenced by the Roman preference for the rectangular shape had much in common with some of those of the

Richard Sheppard's drawing of the last phase of settlement at Dunston's Clump with dwelling, sheds and sheepfold. Trent & Peak Archaeological Trust Transactions of the Thoroton Society of Nottinghamshire 91 (1987).

supposed Saxon conquerors. It may have been the case that British and Saxon traditions combined to create a new generation of rural buildings: timber halls and huts with sunken floors. The Saxon settlers have often been regarded as the founders of our English villages – but there is little cause to accept this claim. Farmsteads and hamlets were established at new and established sites and some small villages existed. These villages bore little resemblance to those of today. They lacked form or structure and stood as random collections of small farm buildings scattered loosely amongst their paddocks. Features like high streets and greens were lacking and most clusters of rural dwellings were hamlets rather than villages.

Several excavated sites seem each to have accommodated an extended family, perhaps comprising a patriarch and his dependent relatives. Such settlements typically contained both halls and huts. The halls were rectangular buildings with walls of upright posts or planks. Internally they were often divided by a timber cross wall to create a large and a small room, and doors were placed facing each other in the sides of the long walls. These buildings resemble the Romano-British farmsteads found at places like Dunston's Clump. The smaller huts echo buildings from the Saxon homelands in the Low Countries and Denmark. They ranged in size from about 10 feet by 7 feet (3 m by 2 m) to about 26 feet by 16 feet (8 m by 5 m). The floors of these buildings were scooped out to form shallow pits and the tent-like roof of thatch and rafters could be supported by a trio of

Reconstructions of buildings from the sixth- to eighth-century Saxon settlements excavated at Chalton in Hampshire. After R. Warmington with the permission of Medieval Archaeology.

internal posts. It is possible that floor boards covered the hollowed storage place beneath and some at least of these subsidiary buildings were used as workshops for weaving and potting. Equally, the presence of the floor pit would have allowed the boards above to remain dry and suitable for storing produce, such as grains.

Various Dark Age hamlet and village settlements have been excavated, one of the most recent projects being at Heslerton in the Vale of Pickering. Around 500 BC a settlement was established on the edge of the vast marshes which then filled the centre of the Vale. This centre prospered and grew, in a straggling manner, surviving right through the Roman occupation. During the deterioration in climate associated with the later phases of Roman rule this damp site became even damper and meanwhile a community of Saxons – perhaps Anglians from southern Denmark – joined the indigenous people, introducing new pottery and the sunken-floored huts.

By around AD 450 the waterlogging of the site urged the abandonment of the settlement – now a thousand years old and unusually venerable. About this time a new settlement was established beside a stream on higher, firmer ground about half a mile (1 km) to the south. Here the buildings were of the characteristic Dark Age types: halls and huts with scooped-out floors. The halls were substantial timber-framed dwellings measuring up to 30 feet by 15 feet (10 m by 5 m), some of the larger ones having two

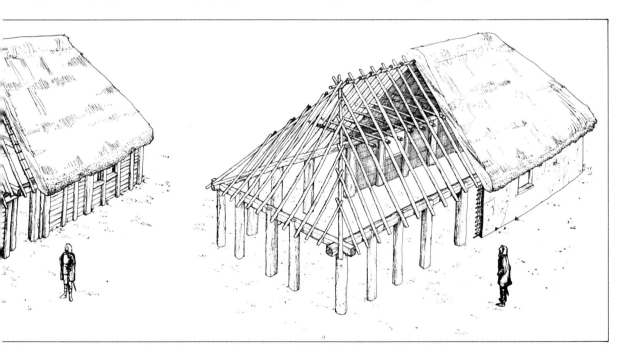

storeys and planked floors. Their main walls were composed of pairs of planks set upright in the ground. The huts were more modest, covering areas of about 12 feet by 10 feet (4 m by 3 m) with floor pits around 20 in (½ m) deep; items of spinning and weaving equipment were found in some pits.

The cemetery of the community lay about 400 yards (365 m) from the homes and adopted the site of a Bronze Age barrow complex, the ancient mounds perhaps still being regarded with reverence. Whatever headway Christianity may have made amongst the countryfolk under the Empire, paganism now predominated. Some people were cremated, their remains being buried in earthenware urns, a practice common in the Saxon homelands. Most corpses were buried, some in crude coffins but some being tossed into pits and lying in distorted positions. Pagan beliefs are evidenced by the provision of grave goods for use in the afterlife: broochs, necklaces, weapons and even a bronze-bound bucket. High levels of infant mortality are characteristic of peasant societies, but infants must have been

Three possible reconstructions of a Saxon building at Cowdery's Down in Hampshire by S.T. James. From the excavated groundplan the structures above the ground could have had any of the forms shown. The Archaeological Journal. Royal Archaeological Institute.

buried or cremated beyond the cemetery. A study of the human remains shows that the average life expectancy for those who survived childhood here was a modest thirty to forty years.

The Dark Age people of Heslerton were peasant farmers who cultivated wheat, rye, barley and flax, used oxen to draw their ploughs and had pony-sized riding horses. Sheep, cattle and pigs were reared and the diet was supplemented by fishing and by hunting with hounds.

Several other Dark Age sites have been excavated in England. At Cowdery's Down, near Basingstoke, a complicated sequence of very impressive timber halls developed: the illustrations below show reconstructions of how one of these halls may have appeared. At West Stow in Suffolk a small community occupied a rather uninviting site early in the fifth century and a hamlet composed of halls and sunken-floored huts developed and endured until the seventh century. During its occupation six halls and thirty-four sunken huts were built, though not all were inhabited at the same time. The hamlet could have accommodated four extended

families, each family having a timber hall and a few ancillary huts. Today the painstaking reconstruction of the buildings provides the visitor with a unique experience of Dark Age life.

Although the shadowy chroniclers of the Dark Age describe titanic struggles which culminated, after various advances and retreats, in the ascendancy of the Saxons and the partial annihilation of the indigenous Romano-British people in England, archaeology paints a different picture. Although a few decrepit western hillforts were hastily refurbished around the time of the Roman collapse, the farmsteads, hamlets and small villages of Arthurian England were undefended and traditional farming pursuits continued amidst the chaos and uncertainties of a land where organisation had collapsed and each community and family subsisted as best they could.

It has recently been estimated that a swollen Romano-British population of up to five million souls absorbed a mere 10,000 Saxon immigrants. Although the immigrants were far too few to conquer outright they did exert an influence on the demoralised indigenous communities which was quite disproportionate to their numbers. Many of the presumed 'Saxon' settlements probably accommodated a British majority population, but

Reconstructed Saxon dwellings, including these 'halls', can be explored at West Stow in Suffolk. Richard Muir.

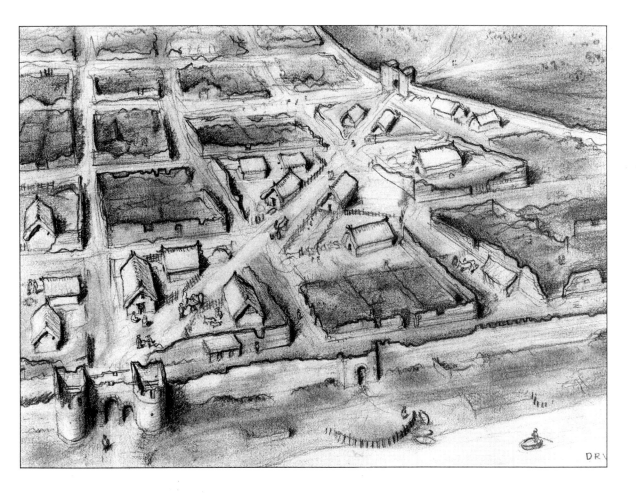

gradually the dialect of the incomers gained ascendancy. Roman institutions withered and England developed new outlooks. These focused not on Rome but on a North Sea cultural arena which had much less sophisticated commerce and organisation. For most people, the struggle for subsistence in an ailing countryside clouded any grander visions. Contrary to popular belief, the Saxons did not make the English landscape, but inherited one whose agricultural foundations were laid in distant times but which was now battered and decaying.

At Heslerton, the village founded around AD 500 was abandoned after about two centuries of occupation. It seems likely that the families migrated to a new settlement established around the church at West Heslerton. Throughout England similar shifts were taking place, marking the beginning of a vital new chapter in the history of the countryside.

A reconstruction of the south-east corner of Lincoln in Saxon times by David Vale. Roman buildings and defences are decaying but the street grid is still recognisable. Thatched Saxon dwellings have been erected and a new routeway runs diagonally across the Roman grid between two Roman gates. Friends of Lincoln Archaeological Research and Excavation.

CHAPTER EIGHT

The Time of Alfred: the Hidden Revolution

WHILE THE YEARS BETWEEN THE Roman withdrawal and the Viking raids are dark and mysterious, those which followed can be compared to a murky dawn. It now seems certain that in the centuries preceding the Norman conquest a combination of revolutionary changes affected our countryside and the foundations of agricultural landscapes which would persist in some places for more than a thousand years were established. However, we still have much to learn about the precise appearance of the vistas through which King Alfred (871–99), his ancestors, successors and their Viking opponents rode. Despite the conflicts and carnage of the middle and late Saxon centuries this was a period of gradual expansion and rehabilitation during which countrysides abandoned or decaying after the collapse of the villa system were often recolonised. Even so, it is unlikely that the population levels of the Roman heyday were approached by the time of the Norman conquest – indeed, in 1066 there may even have been fewer countryfolk in England than were here some two thousand years earlier.

Apart from the information which archaeology provides, our main sources are contemporary literature and art. There are useful drawings which depict peasant activities rather than countrysides, while the literature includes outlines of secular and religious history, laws and charters. Although the land charters sometimes include the rural features which could be encountered in a perambulation of the estate boundaries concerned, we have only the briefest glimpses of the appearance and management of the countryside. Nobody thought it necessary to record the look of the land for the edification of future generations; perhaps the tiny literate minority considered that everybody knew such things and that the landscape always had been and always would be much the same.

Interesting little insights are provided in two of the Laws of King Ine of Wessex, recorded around 690:

A churl's [yeoman's] holding must be fenced both in winter and summer. If not and a neighbour's beast strays in through the gap, the churl has no claim; let him drive the beast out and suffer the loss.

If churls have a meadow in common, or other partible land to fence, and some have fenced their part but some have not, and [stray cattle] eat up their common crops or grass, those who own the unfenced part shall go, and compensate for the damage the other, who have fenced their part. Then [those who neglected fencing] shall ask from the owners of the cattle such amends as may be right. If, however, any beast breaks through the hedges, and its owner cannot, or will not control it, he who finds it in his field may take it and slay it. The owner shall take its hide and flesh, and lose the rest.

When a man destroys a tree in a wood by fire, and it becomes known who did it, he shall pay the full fine. He shall pay 60 shillings, because the fire is a thief. If he fells very many trees in a wood, and it later becomes manifest, he shall pay for three trees, each with 30 shillings. He need not pay for more, be they as many as they may. For an axe is an informer, and not a thief.

If, however, a man cut down a tree that 30 swine may stand under, and it becomes manifest, he shall pay 60 shillings.

These laws show that in Kent, and surely elsewhere, timber trees were regarded as valuable resources. They suggest that livestock were privately owned and that the countryside contained privately owned hedged fields and other fields which were held by the community in common – meadows and (probably) ploughlands are indicated. We also learn of the conflict between communal and individual interests in the countryside – the shirkers who neglect their fences and the losses which may result.

Occasionally it is possible to chart the boundaries of Saxon estates across the modern countryside. Charter boundary perambulations mention specific features of the estates concerned and these fragments of information combine to give us a picture of rural land uses. For example, the landmarks mentioned successively in a royal grant of land at Madeley in Staffordshire to the Bishop of Winchester in 975 are: the wood of the 'witan' or counsellors; the wood where poles are cut; a ford; the heathen swamp; a thorn hedge; a way; a stream where watercress grows; a dyke; a wide marsh; a marshy stream; a reedy moor; a heathery pasture; a great woodland oak, and so back to the wood of the witan. This gives us a picture of a rather soggy locality but does not tell us anything very surprising about the countryside of a thousand years ago. However, when large numbers of such charters are analysed a broader picture emerges.

The distinguished woodland historian, Oliver Rackham, has analysed the countryside as depicted by Saxon charters. The charters are numerous for Wessex and the West Midlands, fewer for the North and rare in the eastern parts of England which were under Danish control. Together they mention a total of 14,342 rural objects. Hedged fields were numerous and there are 378 mentions of hedgerows. Woods are mentioned 384 times – 471 times if place-names indicating woodland are also included – and there is also evidence that some of the heathland pastures of Roman times had reverted to woodland as grazing pressure was reduced by the Dark Age catastrophes. His conclusions may surprise some readers: 'Most charters show that England has altered surprisingly little in the last thousand years. They conduct us through a familiar world of rivers, mill streams, ditches, hedges and hedgerow trees, roads, lanes, paths, bridges, heaths, thorns, small named woods, stumps, pits, and old posts.'

Lest these remarks be misconstrued we should remember first that modern agri-business has wiped scores of countrysides bare of all their ancient charm. Second, the charters reveal that semi-derelict and neglected land was frequently found, much of it doubtless land that had been more productive before the Dark Age calamities. Third, marshes, fens, wet meadows and sodden pastures were far more numerous than today, for land drainage was still a localised and primitive craft.

Before venturing further into the Saxon countryside we should consider the political aspects, for it has already been shown that the link between politics and countryside is close and binding. Land worked to serve a market, town or empire differs from land cultivated for peasant subsistence, while political security is normally associated with stable and prosperous agriculture. After the Roman collapse Romanised aristocrats seem to have struggled to maintain unifying institutions but then failed as local and regional tyrants and despots strove for power. In the climates of division and uncertainty which accompanied the Saxon settlement countryfolk turned to introspection and self-sufficiency and local control seems to have passed to minor patriarchs. Gradually a series of regional kingdoms began to gell, several of them roughly coinciding with Iron Age tribal territories. In England the emerging rulers generally had Saxon names and claimed Saxon pedigrees for, in some uncertain manner, power had passed to leaders of the unsophisticated but adaptable settlers and away from the refined but demoralised indigenous elite. As one dynasty triumphed over another progress towards the unification of an English kingdom was made, but the progress was checked by the Viking invasions of the ninth and tenth centuries.

Previously, however, the re-establishment of Christianity, with the arrival of St Augustine in 597 to restore English kingdoms to the Christian fold, unleashed forces which now appear to have exerted an enormous influence on the organisation of the countryside. It appears that at the time of the conversion most countrysides in England and Wales lay in great estates. These estates, some of which could date back to Roman or earlier times, were self-sufficient in most country products, could be divided internally into different cells, each one specialising in a separate field of production, and the whole estate rendered produce to a 'caput' or head manor where the local estate owner and potentate might have his court. Some estates were compact, but some had outlying portions of common or woodland grazings. The first churches to be established in the conversion period were minsters, staffed by a body of clergy whose members preached and sought converts in the territory around. Such mother churches were often established on royal estates where the literate clergy could perform useful duties for the king. Subsequently, proprietorial churches were established by other landowners on their own estates, and in this way the estate coincided with the new parish.

In 956 King Edwy granted a great estate at Southwell in Nottinghamshire to Oscetel, Archbishop of York. The estate embraced four old manors and the boundaries of these manors correspond very closely to those of four present-day parishes. Perambulations of the four manors were provided in the charter concerned and their boundaries can be followed through the modern countryside using the thousand-year-old description even though landmarks formed by trees have disappeared. Here is an example:

> These are the boundaries belonging to Normanton; from the River Greet to the corner of land where the dill grows; along the enclosure to the brook, then to the valley; along the valley all the time by the headland to the Leen Brook; from thence to the hedge, all the time by the hedge to the old paved way; along the paved way then back to the Greet. . . .

In the middle centuries of the Saxon era the lowland countryside experienced a major transformation. In the archaeological record this is marked by the desertion of scores of farmsteads, hamlets and small villages. At the same time new settlements were being formed, apparently sucking in the populations from the surrounding countryside. This was the most formative period in the history of the English village, for many of the dwelling clusters that gelled endure as villages to the present day. The new centres frequently had churches – did the church attract the dwellings, did the reverse attraction occur, or was the whole process stage-managed by the local estate owners?

The remarkable change in the settlement pattern was accompanied in many places by a complete reorganisation of farming patterns. The earlier Dark Age farmers inherited networks of ancient and Roman fields and there is nothing to suggest that they changed them. These fields might form brickwork patterns, fan out from a farmstead or form clusters with irregular shapes so that the countryside was a patchwork of enclosures hemmed by hedges, ditches and wattle fences. Now, however, old boundaries were destroyed and ploughland was gathered together in vast arable fields. These fields were subdivided into blocks or furlongs and the furlongs into gently curving ribbons of ground known as lands, selions or strips. The use of a plough with a mouldboard behind the share allowed the sod to be turned to one side, and this device was employed to ridge up the land into corduroy patterns which assisted drainage. Within each young community a peasant family tenanted a number of strips and these were dispersed around the two, three or more great open ploughfields. They were also allocated shares in common meadow land and rights of grazing in the commons beyond the ploughlands and meadows, while privately held pastures often endured around the homesteads or between the open fields, meadows and commons.

This reorganisation of the countryside did not affect all areas and was not achieved at once but continued into the years following the Norman conquest. In many places the changes were never accomplished and ancient countryside patterns persisted. In such places strips were accommodated within existing fields and these fields were relatively small and shared by few tenants. A contrast developed between the reorganised countrysides, with growing villages set in the hearts of little empires of open ploughlands, meadows, pastures and commons, and ancient countrysides which looked much as they had in Roman times, with scattered farmsteads and hamlets, deep, winding lanes and rich, curving hedgerows. Even today one can recognise the differences inherited from this period, with recognisable expanses of ancient countryside surviving in parts of Kent, Essex, Norfolk, the north, the Welsh Marches and the south-west, where the new open-field organisation made much less headway than in its Midlands heartland.

The role of the church in these transformations is uncertain, though the appearance of villages with village churches coincided with the agricultural changes. When St Augustine landed with his mission and interpreters in Thanet in 597, England was a largely pagan country although monks of the Celtic church operated in Cornwall, Wales and the north while Christian congregations may also have survived in Yorkshire. The conversion was swift, if not without setbacks, because the missionaries made it their priority to convert the rulers of the English kingdoms. By the eighth century seventeen dioceses were established in England, numerous minsters having been established in the preceding century. Typically, these pioneer churches may have existed as a collection of timber buildings set within a hedge or palisade. Some minster churches were of stone; examples survive at Breedon in Leicestershire and Brixworth in Northamptonshire. Occasionally, the building was imposing and illumin-

The construction of the first stone-built church of St Peter at Northampton in the years around AD 700. Just above the ox cart used for transporting stone is a circular mortar mixer. Northamptonshire County Council.

ated by stained-glass windows, as was the case with the important minster at Jarrow. The early church cultivated its contacts with the aristocrats controlling Saxon society and the Christian message circulated freely to churls, bond tenants and slaves only when local magnates provided estate or parish churches. This is known to have happened in several specific cases after a 'gesith' or landowner had offered hospitality to an itinerant priest and had been encouraged to found a small chapel or oratory. He might, at first, have been primarily concerned to provide for the needs of his own family, but as the church became open to his servants, tenants and estate workers so a new parish was in the process of forming. Sometimes the church building was preceded by the erection of a cross which formed a venue for preaching by itinerant clergy from a minster, with the dead being buried in the sanctified ground surrounding the cross. When the church was erected this cross might be buried in the church foundations or else the church might be erected over the cross.

Most estate churches were modest buildings, rectangular and narrow, but relatively lofty. Those that were originally built of timber were generally rebuilt in stone, though towers did not become common until the tenth century. During the Danish wars of the ninth century the richly endowed minsters perished, although the humble estate churches had little to interest the plunderers. By the close of the Saxon period lowland England was well served by parish churches. We do not know how many existed but shortly after the Norman conquest there were about 400 churches in the two Kentish dioceses of Canterbury and Rochester alone.

A number of Saxon churches survive, a few of them more or less intact. Evidence of Saxon work, often only surviving in fragmentary form, can be

The late tenth-century Saxon church tower at Earls Barton in Northamptonshire. The parapet is much more recent but the tower displays Saxon decoration. The Saxon church largely consisted of the tower, perhaps built as a family chapel by the local lord. Richard Muir.

Opposite: *reconstruction drawings by Mary Haynes of the evolution of Rivenhall Church. The progression is from top left to bottom right. The Saxon timber church was succeeded by a substantial stone building built with hardly any foundations. The rounded apse was added in the Norman period. The tower was built at the end of the fifteenth century and collapsed in 1714. By courtesy of Dr Warwick Rodwell.*

found in 400 British churches, but there are a great many more places where all traces of the original Saxon church have vanished. Readers will appreciate that the typical old church displays architecture in two or three different styles but only on rare occasions where excavation is possible can we appreciate just how many rebuildings an old church experienced, one founded in Saxon times having up to a dozen major building episodes in the course of its long life. A particularly informative church was explored at Rivenhall in Essex by Warwick and Kirsty Rodwell.

Here a villa and its estate survived the traumas of the Roman collapse. The main domestic building was modified in the fifth century and in the next century a timber hall was built in the courtyard of the stone villa, jutting out at a right angle from the villa's wall. Later a new hall was built just to the north of the old villa. Although no village developed here local power remained centred on the site of the old Roman villa and in the tenth century a timber chapel was built over an infilled cellar which had underlain the south wing of the villa. Early in the following century the simple timber church was demolished and replaced by a stone church with a nave and chancel, the ruined villa being quarried to provide the building materials. Subsequently the church experienced several other rebuildings, one of them necessitated by the collapse of the tower in 1714, which subsided into the foundation trench of a projected but abandoned mid-fourteenth-century tower. Until the excavations began there was no clue that Rivenhall church had such a long and interesting history and that a Dark Age hall and a Roman villa were its ancestors – indeed, the Roman cellar above which the church was built may have been used for some form of worship.

The reconstruction drawing of the Saxon church at Raunds in Northamptonshire portrays a typical small but lofty building of the period. Excavations have shown that this church was erected around 1050 and demolished shortly afterwards when its site was commandeered by a Norman manor house. It had been preceded by a much smaller church also

The Saxon church at Furnell's Manor, Raunds, as it existed around AD 100. The drawing, by P. Goff, is based on excavation and comparisons with surviving churches of the period. Northamptonshire County Council.

94

consisting of a simple nave and chancel, which may have originally been built to serve a family rather than a community. Around 1000 the nature of the service had changed. Previously the priest and congregation had gathered around the altar to celebrate the Mass together, but in the new church the ritual adopted would have been different, with the congregation acting as spectators as the priest celebrated the Mass with his back to the congregation before an altar set against the wall of the chancel.

With the establishment of new villages, churches and open-field farming the building blocks of the medieval countryside were gradually falling into place. However, these innovations were achieved against a background of strife. The West Saxon Annals record that in 789 'King Beorhtric of Wessex took to wife Eadburg, daughter of Offa: and in his days came first three ships; and the reeve rode thereto, and wished to drive them to the King's town, because he knew not what they were: and they slew him; and those were the first ships of Danish men that sought the land of England . . .' In fact, these Viking raiders may not have been Danes, for another version of the account claims that they came from the vicinity of Hardanger fjord in Norway. In 793 the monastery at Lindisfarne was plundered and an attack on Jarrow monastery took place in the following year. Viking piracy dominated affairs in the century that followed and in the final third of this century pragmatic raiding gave way to systematic attempts at conquest. Eastern England between the Tees and the Thames estuary was occupied by Danish warriors and settlers and became 'Danelaw', where Danish law and tenure held sway. However, in the three final decades of the ninth century Alfred, arguably the greatest English king, led a resistance movement which prevented the total domination of England by Danish and Norwegian rulers. Ultimately neither the English nor the Vikings emerged victorious. At the start of the eleventh century the burden of danegeld, collected to buy off Viking raiders, was crippling the English kingdom and in 1016 Cnut, son of a Danish king, took the English throne. Harold, the last English king, was partly Danish and in his last victorious battle he defeated a powerful Viking invasion force at Stamford Bridge in 1066.

It is not at all easy to recognise differences between countrysides controlled by the Danes and the English. The negative impact of Viking raiding was considerable. It exterminated most of the early English monasteries and thus accelerated the rise of the estate church over the minster. In the areas which they occupied the Danes were no more than a small but dominant minority in the population but their presence does seem to have affected the hierarchical and authoritarian English societies, for a much higher proportion of free peasants appeared in the territory of old Danelaw. In England as a whole, however, the Viking wars seem to

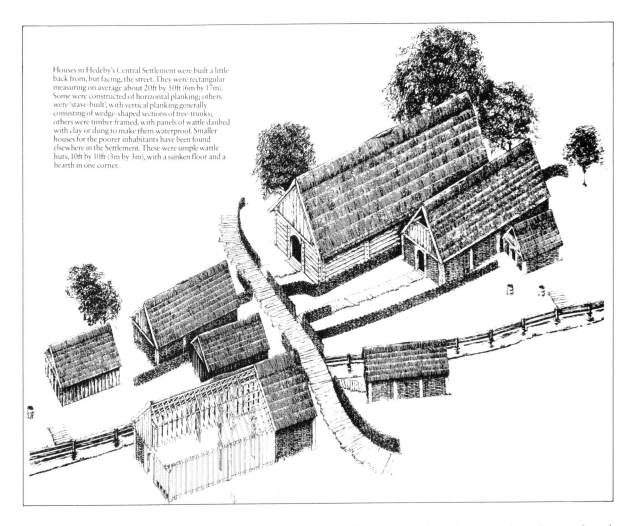

Houses in Hedeby's Central Settlement were built a little
back from, but facing, the street. They were rectangular
measuring on average about 20ft by 50ft (6m by 17m).
Some were constructed of horizontal planking; others
were 'stave-built', with vertical planking generally
consisting of wedge-shaped sections of tree-trunks;
others were timber framed, with panels of wattle daubed
with clay or dung to make them waterproof. Smaller
houses for the poorer inhabitants have been found
elsewhere in the Settlement. These were simple wattle
huts, 10ft by 10ft (3m by 3m), with a sunken floor and a
hearth in one corner.

*A reconstruction of dwellings
from the Viking homelands at
Hedeby in Denmark. Some
were built of horizontal
planking, others of vertical
staves and others still were of
timber-framing with wattle
and daub panels.*

have paved the way for feudalism as churls, who were heavily taxed and
obliged to render military service, lost status and became increasingly
dependent on their lords or 'thegns'. The Danes renamed many of the
places in eastern and northern England and contributed many new words
to their dialects. For all this, distinctively Danish countrysides were not
created although the Vikings did play an important role in shaping
development at sea and in the towns.

When the Vikings sacked Lindisfarne, Alcuin, who was master of the
monastic school at York, thought it impossible that the raiders could have
accomplished the long and hazardous crossing of the North Sea. This was
curious since the Saxons had a seafaring tradition, many of their forebears
originating in what were now the Danish homelands. The burial ground of
the East Anglian dynasty at Sutton Hoo may contain more than the two
known ship burials, the famous excavated example revealing a massive
rowing boat some 95 feet (29 m) long with a towering 12 feet (3.8 m) prow

but a draft of only about 2 feet (0.6 m). Such a sea-going vessel of the seventh century could also navigate in shallow estuarine and riverine waters. Viking ships embodied several improvements on the Sutton Hoo design: an external keel giving greater stability, a mast set forward of amidships to carry a square sail, a tiller and rowlocks cut into the hull, the slots being sealed by shutters when the boat was not being rowed. Boats recovered virtually intact in the Viking homelands provide a detailed understanding of the construction and capabilities of these ships. King Alfred realised the need to challenge the Vikings at sea and created a fleet of several hundred ships which provided a measure of security during the ninth century. The *Anglo Saxon Chronicle* records that in 896 the king 'had long ships built to oppose the Danish warships. They were almost twice as long as the others. Some had 60 oars, some more. They were both swifter and steadier and also higher than others. They were built neither on the Frisian or on the Danish pattern, but as it seemed to him himself that they could be most useful.'

The second prong of Alfred's strategy involved the establishment of a series of fortified towns. As we have seen, town life declined in the latter part of the Roman administration and although a very run-down form of occupation may have continued at a few centres like London and York, many of the Roman towns were deserted. Archaeologists working at several town sites find a layer of black soil intervening between the Roman and post-Roman urban levels, suggesting that debris accumulated in empty streets and that farmers worked amongst the ruins. Later a few new towns appeared, though they differed considerably from the Roman model. Ipswich was founded in the seventh century as commerce began to revive and it expanded to cover an area of about 125 acres (50 ha). It was a trading port with an important wine trade and pottery industry. Other kingdoms developed their own trading ports, with Hamwith near Southampton in Wessex being the most important example. Such towns may have been founded by kings as their personal trading centres, with the kings distributing imports as gifts in return for taxes and tribute rendered by their subjects. Meanwhile urban life very gradually revived at the more important Roman towns, which retained their positions as route centres on roads which had never been abandoned. By the ninth century the re-establishment of a market trading system fostered the appearance of more towns.

In his wars with the Danes Alfred came to admire the strategic importance of the Danish fortified camps, which provided secure refuges and the launching pads for new attacks. The Danes developed fortified boroughs in Danelaw at Derby, Leicester, Lincoln, Nottingham and Stamford. Alfred and his heirs imitated the Danish boroughs by creating a series of fortified towns or *burhs* to protect the borders and heartlands of Wessex, each *burh* the centre of a military district with the population of the *burh* being responsible for manning its defences and campaigning in its district. The *burhs* were a mixed collection. Some were new foundations, others, like Exeter and Chichester, were revived Roman centres. Some were not towns so much as fortresses guarding market places and a few, like Chisbury Camp in Wiltshire, were Iron Age hillforts. Some had carefully planned street lay-outs, as at Winchester, while others had rambling streets. Some endure as important towns, some as country market towns, some as villages, like Langport in Somerset, and a few failed completely. The best preserved examples are Cricklade, Wallingford and Wareham, all having as ramparts the enclosing rectangular earthbank defences which protected a gridwork of streets defining property blocks reminiscent of the Roman *insulae*. Within two decades of Alfred's death no part of Wessex lay more than twenty miles from a *burh*, and although no new *burhs* of any standing were founded after 920 the urban revival continued and flourished during the tenth century.

Our most detailed understanding of urban life derives from excavations undertaken in 1976–81 in the Coppergate section of York. A revival of urban life had already occurred when the town fell to Vikings in 866. Renamed as 'Jorvik', the old Roman fortress city had its street patterns redefined, its walls repaired and extended, and it emerged as an important trading city of the Viking commercial arena. Despite its vibrancy and bustle Jorvik fell far below Roman standards of organisation and cleanliness. The excavations explored the area of Viking Jorvik in the vicinity of the streets known as Pavement and Coppergate, the latter name meaning the street of the cup-makers. Property boundaries survived from Viking times until the eighteenth century with the Viking buildings being set parallel or at right angels to Pavement in long narrow houseplots running back from the street, with street frontages of about 18 feet (5.5 m). Narrow alleys of closely packed dwellings ran back from the main streets.

Two forms of construction were used to build the rectangular timber dwellings.

On the Coppergate street frontage there were rectangular buildings about 23 feet long by 15 feet wide (7 by 4.5 m) which were built of wattle woven around upright posts. Their floors were of earth and their roofs of thatch or turf. They had no chimneys and large hearths of clay edged in limestone blocks or in old Roman tiles were placed in the centre of the living rooms. Large storage or rubbish pits were actually dug within the living area and were presumably covered over with planks. These dwellings were occupied by craftsmen, including metalworkers, coin-makers, and glassmakers.

After the expulsion of the last Viking king, Erik Bloodaxe, from York in 954 the mixed English and Scandinavian population remained but radical changes in building techniques followed. The new Coppergate buildings surrounded sunken basements which were dug out to depths of almost 5 ft (1.5 m) and their walls were built of horizontal oak planks supported by upright posts. With the greater part of the living area being below ground level, the roof lines must have been very low as there is no evidence of upper storeys. These unusual dwellings served as homes and workshops and were occupied by craftsmen, including jewellers working in amber and jet and wood turners producing platters and bowls who may have been the cuppers who gave Coppergate its name.

Oak and birch were cut to provide the main structural timbers and alder, beech, birch and hazel were used for the brushwood floorings and for light fencing and wattle. Building timbers were attacked by woodworm and powder-post beetle and the earthfast ends of posts soon rotted in the

Above and overleaf: scenes from the reconstruction of Viking Jorvik. Jorvik Viking Centre, photograph by Mike S. Duffy. Above: a domestic scene around the hearth.

water-logged ground. Each dwelling endured for only about a generation before it became derelict, when a new house was built upon the decaying floors of the old.

The sights and the smells of Viking York must have been reminiscent of those of unmodernised Middle Eastern towns. Craftsmen and traders sold their wares from open and lean-to street-side stalls – bone-carvers, wood turners, tub-makers, leather-workers, jewellers, shoe-makers, all plying their wares. Conditions in and around the crowded alleys were clamorous and squalid. Pig sties and open privies lay in the yards right beside dwellings, polluting the neighbouring wells. Insects swarmed and people played host to a range of internal parasites: eggs of two types of parasitic worms were recognised by the excavators. The unglamorous but informative excavation of privies shows that as well as staples like oats and bran the Jorvik diet also included a range of wild birds including rarities such as the puffin and the red kite, the latter bird being a common scavenger in medieval cities. Cattle, sheep, goats and pigs were bought 'on the hoof' and slaughtered in the backyards. As in Roman times, oysters were very popular and cockles and mussels were also gathered. Sea fish including cod, herring, haddock and flat fish were imported, with pike, roach, bream, perch, eels and salmon being caught in the local rivers.

The poor standards of sanitation in the bustling trading centre and the eruption of epidemics which were common in Dark Age times helped to depress life expectancy. Only one person in ten lived to enjoy a sixtieth birthday, more than half the women who survived adolescence died before reaching the age of thirty-five and a quarter of the population died in childhood. The stench and filth of Jorvik contrasted with the luxuries arriving at the river port from distant places – with wines from the Rhineland, silks from the Middle East and costly oils and spices coming from still more distant places. Around 1000 Jorvik was described as being 'full of treasures of merchants coming from many places'. After Erik Bloodaxe was expelled from Jorvik, the prosperity of the Anglo-Danish city continued under English rule. Now the Jorvik Viking Centre offers visitors a remarkable opportunity to experience the sights, sounds and smells of the tenth-century York, with reconstructed buildings erected above the foundations of their originals.

Although we can begin to picture the countrysides of Saxon England, those of Wales and Scotland are more elusive. It is likely that Wales was divided into great estates, some of them centred on old Roman strongholds, and that these estates were subdivided into subordinate territories, each with a hamlet at its core and each rendering a special form of tribute to the estate centre. In Wales the Roman occupation did not transform the fabric of the native society, while Christianity, which was established in Roman times, endured through the troubled centuries which followed. In Scotland agriculture was established in low-lying coastal and island situations in Neolithic and Bronze Age times. However, in the rugged interior the native Scots pine-dominated forests seem to have endured largely intact through prehistoric and Roman times. In the centuries following the Roman withdrawal from England the clearance of woodland in the lowlands of the north-east may be evidenced by the many place-names which begin with 'Pit'. The word, which may have denoted a farmstead or land-holding in the lost language of the Picts, would have been in use until the Pictish nation was conquered and absorbed into Kenneth McAlpin's Scottish kingdom in 843. During the Viking era Shetland, Orkney, the Western Isles and the western seaboard of Scotland received many Norwegian settlers and around this time there is also evidence of substantial woodland clearance in the uplands of southern Scotland.

Those who tersely recorded the brief outlines of pre-conquest history were concerned with great men, their dynasties and battles and with landmarks in ecclesiastical history. Even today it is easy to visualise the period in terms of epic conflicts and to lose sight of the fact that the countrysides of the time were created by the arduous toil of ordinary people. Just occasionally one may find a piece of contemporary writing which reminds us of this simple fact. The Colloquy of Abbot Aelfric of Eynsham, written around AD 1000, consists of a series of dialogues created to assist students of Latin:

> TEACHER: What dost thou say, ploughman? How dost thou go about thy work?
>
> PLOUGHMAN: Lo, my lord, hard work have I. I go out at daybreak urging my oxen to the field, and I yoke them to the plough. However stark the winter, I dare not lurk at home, for fear of my lord. But when my oxen are yoked, and the share and the coulter are fastened to the plough, each day I must plough a full acre, or more.
>
> TEACHER: Hast thou any comrade?
>
> PLOUGHMAN: I have a boy, urging on the oxen with the goad, who, too, is now hoarse with cold and shouting.
>
> TEACHER: What else dost thou?
>
> PLOUGHMAN: Verily, I do still more. I must fill the mangers of the oxen with hay, and water them, and bear out their dung.
>
> TEACHER: Oh! Oh! Great work it is.
>
> PLOUGHMAN: Yea, Sir, great work it is, for I am not free.

A Trip Through Domesday England

OUR VISIONS OF THE SAXON countryside are based in part upon incidental mentions of rural features bequeathed by writers who saw no need to record word pictures of commonplace scenes. The reader may well assume that the compilation of Domesday Book in 1086 embodied the first attempt to provide future generations with a detailed description of the exact appearance of the landscapes of England. However, one cannot think of another book whose contents and purpose are so widely misunderstood. Only when we appreciate the true nature of Domesday Book can we begin to glean worthwhile insights from its pages.

With the defeat of the English army at Battle near Hastings in 1066 England fell under the control of William of Normandy. This illegitimate son of Robert, Duke of Normandy, had succeeded through a ruthless tenacity and a large measure of good luck in securing not only the Dukedom of Normandy but also the crown of England. The remainder of his life was devoted to the struggle to safeguard his conquests. In England he superimposed a centralised government upon the authoritarian yet devolved Saxon system of administration. All such governments depend upon information and Domesday Book was, in large part, a monumental attempt to record what William's vassals held, the value of their estates and what taxes and obligations were owed to him. The mere fact that the vast survey was accomplished demonstrated to one and all the might and pervasive nature of William's government.

A description of the exercise which is much more reliable than many later interpretations was provided in the *Anglo-Saxon Chronicle*, which told how, at the end of 1085, the king

> had important deliberations and exhaustive discussions with his council about this land, how it was peopled, and with what sort of men. Then he sent his men all over England into every shire to ascertain how many hundreds of 'hides' of land there were in every shire, and how much land and livestock the king himself owned in the country, and what annual dues were lawfully his from each shire.

This entry summarises the motives for the survey but is unduly flattering (or pessimistic) when it adds:

> So thoroughly did he have the enquiry carried out that there was not a single 'hide' [around 120 acres/50 ha], not one virgate of land [around 30 acres/ 12 ha], not even – it is shameful to record it, but it did not seem shameful to him to do – not even one ox, nor one cow, nor one pig which escaped notice in his survey.

The English, hostile to most things Norman, and usually with good reason, associated the survey with the horrors of the Last Judgement and so the great survey came to be known as Domesday Book.

Contemporary returns from Ely Abbey summarise how the evidence was recorded:

> They enquired what the manor was called; who held it in the time of King Edward; who holds it now; how many hides there are; how many hides in demesne [land worked directly for the lord of the manor] and how many belonging to the men; how many villeins [bond tenants]; how many cottars [lowly bond tenants]; how many slaves [slavery was a Saxon rather than a Norman institution]; how many free men; how many sokemen [yeomen]; how much woodland; how much meadow; how much pasture; how many mills; how many fisheries; how much has been added to, or taken from the estate; what was it worth then [in King Edward's time]; what is it worth now, and how much each freeman and sokeman had or has . . .

Great Domesday book in its binding dating from 1953. Public Record Office.

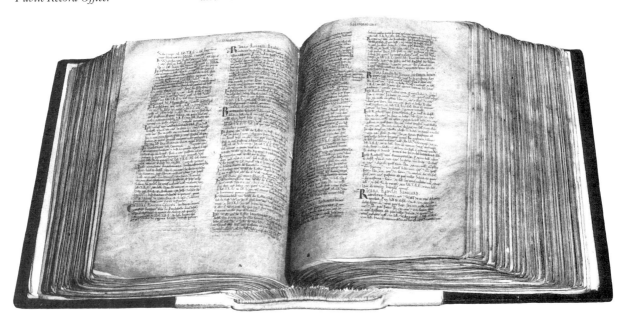

In fact most entries answer only some of these questions and many contain very little information, but to see how the formula was applied (and converted into a sort of Latin shorthand) we can relate it to a particular entry:

> In Bassingbourn [Cambridgeshire] the Bishop holds 1 hide and 2½ virgates. There is land for 3 ploughs. In demesne 1 hide, and 1 plough is there. There are 1 villein and 4 bordars [bordars had a lower status than villeins] with 1 plough and there could be another. There, 2 mills yielding 20 shillings. Meadow for 1 plough. It is worth 60 shillings. When he received it, 40 shillings. In the time of King Edward, 60 shillings. This land pertained and pertains to the Church of St Peter of Winchester and there was 1 sokeman, the man of Archbishop Stigand, who held half a virgate and he could give and sell it.

From Domesday Book one discovers around 9,300 landlords and churchmen; 23,000 sokemen; 12,000 freemen; and 225,000 bondsmen of different ranks. Since only the heads of families would be listed it is necessary to multiply the Domesday estimates by a factor which allows for family sizes in order to arrive at a figure for the total population; five is conventionally chosen. A generous interpretation of the Domesday figure would give a population in Norman England of around two million, but it is plain that many people escaped the notice of the survey makers. It would be hard to believe that the Domesday population of England was more than three million – and despite the recoveries of the middle and late Saxon periods it was still considerably below the figure of five million produced by recent estimates of the population of the Roman heyday. By 1300 the population had reached its medieval peak of about four to six million.

Domesday England was a land of manors, each manor being worked by peasants to produce an income for their lord. Most lords were foreigners, the majority of English landlords being killed at Hastings, in the local revolts which followed, or otherwise dispossessed. The places mentioned in Domesday Book are manors – estates and not, as people so commonly believe, villages. The mention of a place in Domesday Book is no indication that a village which bears that name today existed in 1086. The manor could be compact and surround a single village, it could contain hamlets and farmsteads but no village, it could divide a village or have outlying fragments or 'berewicks'.

A comparably bulky book could be devoted to describing what Domesday Book does not tell us and how it has been misunderstood, but let us now explore the useful information about the countryside that it contains.

Woodland is sometimes recorded in terms of the number of swine the woods concerned might support, sometimes the length or length and

Much Domesday woodland would have been carefully managed and look like this, with standards towering above coppiced underwood. Richard Muir.

breadth of a wood is given and quite often a wood was completely overlooked. For example, the currently threatened ancient Birkham Wood near Knaresborough existed but was overlooked in an entry which mentioned only a nearby pocket of meadow. The general picture that emerges is of a countryside which was not heavily wooded. Only a loose estimate of the wooded area can be made, expressed, as follows, by Oliver Rackham: 'England was not well wooded even by the standards of the twentieth century, let alone eleventh-century Europe. It had a proportion of woodland between those of modern France (20 per cent of the land) and modern Denmark (9 per cent).'

Cumbria was not covered by the Domesday survey and may well have contained some extensive woods. Elsewhere woods were typically small and, though numerous, they were in no sense wilderness and should be regarded as areas carefully reserved for the production of woodland products. Most manors had at least one small wood where tenants could obtain timber for different uses and some manors had 'outwoods' reserved for the use of the lord. There were no impenetrable forests and most of the larger woods were found close to the well-populated areas, the Weald, the Chilterns and the West Midlands containing substantial and numerous woods. To quote Rackham again: 'Even the bigger wooded areas were not uninhabited wildwood; it was nowhere possible in Norman England to penetrate into woodland further than four miles from some habitation.' (It is possible to do so today following the afforestation of so many attractive upland areas with unsightly plantations of alien conifers.)

Small wooded islands separated by farmland can be seen today in many parts of England that have escaped the clutches of the barley barons, but on closer inspection Domesday woods were rather different to most seen today. First there were no foreign conifers: woods were deciduous with just native yew, holly, juniper and box to provide winter greenery. Chestnut, a Roman introduction, could be found in a few Domesday woods, but there were no sycamores, these invaders of woodland and gardens being introduced in the sixteenth and seventeenth centuries. There were other differences in the tree population which are less easily discovered. Prior to the modern outbreak of Dutch elm disease, elm was tending to invade and dominate some deciduous woods. Research from Epping Forest shows that from Neolithic to early Saxon times this forest was dominated by lime. In the seventh, eighth and ninth centuries selective woodland clearance ended this domination. Lime was gradually replaced by hazel, birch and oak. Then beech gained a strong foothold in the forest with a late appearance and expansion of hornbeam helping to produce the modern oak, birch, beech and hornbeam composition. At the time of Domesday here the lime was still common though declining, hornbeam was not yet evident and beech had only begun to secure a foothold.

Domesday woods were working woods and many produced more income than equivalent areas of ploughland. Trees were allowed to grow tall as standards yielding heavy timber or were coppiced every ten years or so to supply light timber. Often the two systems of management were combined so that tall oak, ash or elm standards towered above a coppiced underwood of elm, ash, hazel or lime. Such woodland vistas are rarely seen today but are always attractive. The underwood provides ample cover for wildlife as the coppiced 'stools' begin to sprout a new crop of leafy poles, while after coppicing the light streaming down through gaps in the canopy of standards allows orchids, bluebells, primroses and oxlips to produce a flush of spring colour.

A frequent component of the Domesday countryside which is very seldom seen today was wood pasture, sometimes recorded specifically in Domesday as *silva pastilis*. In Derbyshire, to cite an extreme example, this sort of countryside covered a quarter of the county. It was produced by a delicate balance between grazing and woodmanship. Trees were normally 'pollarded' or decapitated above the reach of browsing animals where a crop of poles could grow safely, while the spaces between the pollards were grazed by livestock and carpeted in grass or heather. Most wood pasture was common land, sometimes the timber – as well as the grazing – was used by peasants and sometimes the lord controlled the trees. By the time of Domesday, wood pasture, widespread in prehistoric times, may have been in retreat and it was greatly reduced in the centuries which followed. More intensive grazing prevented any tree seedlings from reaching maturity while the enclosure of sections of this countryside by fences or banks which excluded livestock resulted in domination by the tree component. Today parkland with closely-spaced pollards approximates loosely with appearance to wood pasture and heaths where trees are now colonising as a result of reduced grazing pressure by rabbits and sheep resemble another form of this environment. At the time of Domesday there were few English folk who were not familiar with this attractive, rather idyllic sort of scenery, but today few are even aware of its appearance, let alone its former extent. Much of the land recorded as woodland in Domesday was probably really wood pasture, in which case, and contrary to popular belief, true woodland would have been even less extensive and unfamiliar wood pasture even more widespread.

The other forms of pasture in Domesday England existed either in enclosed fields or open commons. The grazed commons included a wide range of environments: downland, acid heaths, northern fells, fens and marshes and coastal saltmarsh. Domesday Book was cursory and erratic in recording pasture even though pasture was a vital component of any

Much in England had not changed greatly between the ninth century when these manuscript paintings were made and 1086. Note the wild swine amongst the pollarded trees, which probably stood in wood pasture. The British Library

farming economy. Rackham guesses that England's 81,000 Domesday ploughs required a haulage force of 648,000 oxen, with one million cattle being directly or indirectly involved with ploughing when cows and their calves are taken into account. There were at least two million sheep and when these livestock figures are related to grazing needs it appears that a good third of England was utilised as grazing land. There is no way of knowing exactly how this grazing was divided between the different forms of open and enclosed land.

A good proportion of livestock had to be supported through the winter months when the pastures were dormant and so a sure supply of winter fodder in the form of hay was essential. This was obtained from meadows which were kept free of livestock until one or two crops of grass had been taken. Domesday Book is more thorough in its recording of meadow land and it is clear that the great majority of communities had access to a meadow even though the fullest use of this vital asset does not seem to have been made. Possibly the concentration of arable farming in open fields was still developing, so that potential meadow land was being 'wasted' as ploughland. Less than a fiftieth of the area of England was devoted to meadow although some places, like Lincolnshire, had a disproportionately high share of it. Probably much of the Domesday meadow land lay in damp riverside commons which were sub-divided into narrow strips or 'doles' with each peasant household having a share in the resource and each manor having part of the meadow in its 'home farm' or demesne.

A little over a third of England was devoted to ploughland. By 1086 much of this ploughland would have been concentrated in vast open ploughfields subdivided into furlongs and strips. In some counties, like Dorset, the arable area covered almost half the land surface, though in

icut in irritacione: secundum die

Above and on the following pages: *although dating from around 1340 the Luttrell Psalter depicts farming practices little changed since Domesday times. The British Library.*

Left: *harrowing the ploughsoil with slingstones being cast at rooks;* opposite: *gathering the sheaves together.*

cooler, damper and hillier regions the potential for cultivation was much less.

Most of the estates listed in Domesday would have contained a village, shared a village or contained more than one village. Information about towns is scanty but it is plain that the revival in town life, which had taken place in the second half of the Saxon period and had been given an impetus with the creation of the *burhs*, was continuing. London was the largest town, containing over 10,000 inhabitants. The other leading towns, perhaps around half the size of London, were Lincoln, Norwich, Thetford, Winchester and York. The towns were administrative and trading centres with craft industries and markets for agricultural produce. There was no really large-scale industry, the main industrial activities being rural iron-working and textiles, lead working in the Pennines, quarrying and salt production from coastal saltings and the Cheshire salt fields.

The overall picture of Domesday England is of an essentially rural land with a well-developed farming economy. Rackham suggests that about 15 per cent of the countryside was wooded, 35 per cent was ploughland, 25 per cent was pasture, with the remaining 25 per cent of the land being divided between grazed common moors, heaths and fens, ground covered by settlement and areas devastated by war. Within this general panorama there was great variation, not only between the regions of upland and lowland, fen and mountain but also within regions. These differences depended upon whether or not the fully-fledged system of open-field farming had been adopted in a locality and the scenic contrasts can be summarised by juxtaposing two imaginary countrysides.

uidit i commota est terra
ontes sicut cera fluxerunt a facie

First let us picture a typical scene in the Midlands where open-field farming has its strongest presence. We see a village of thatched hovels clustered around a stone church with the timber-framed manor house nearby. All the land surrounding the village and the tiny hedged pastures attached to each dwelling is arable. Here there are no hedgerows or houses to relieve the scenery, it is winter and we see two of the enormous fields with their dark ploughsoil exposed. The soil has been turned by the mouldboard of the plough in such a way as to form sinuous ridges, blocks of parallel ridges being grouped together into roughly rectangular furlongs. The ridging assists drainage and provides a small safeguard against adversity, with crops surviving in the furrows between the ridges in drought years or on the crests of the ridges in the wetter times. Seen from afar the scene resembles a great patchwork made of rectangles of brown corduroy. Different furlongs would be planted with wheat, barley, oats and legumes, with shoots of winter-sown wheat giving some furlongs a faintly greenish cast. The third vast field is being rested as fallow. After the harvest the village sheep and cattle are grazed upon the stubble of all the fields and now the fallowing field, which will be grazed again in spring, summer and autumn, is sprouting a self-sown crop of weeds and grasses.

Between the river and the open ploughlands there is a ribbon of meadowland which extends along the floodplain for mile upon mile. In late spring it becomes a shimmering sea of orchids, fritillaries, cowslips and buttercups, while after the hay crops have been cut and dried it is a lush autumn pasture grazed by the village cattle. Small hedged pastures and woods and copses fill the middle distance, while the low hills on the skyline

Above: threshing with a flail.
Opposite: watermills existed
in Domesday England but the
windmill is thought to have
been introduced by returning
crusaders.

are clothed in wood pasture, with many trees forming a darker stipple on the green background. From commons, woods, meadows and ploughlands the muddy trackways and field paths converge upon the village and every dawn the peasants walk out from their homes to perform their allotted tasks like bees from a hive. Ploughmen, cowherds, shepherds, smiths or millers, from the prosperous villein to the most work-laden bordar and impoverished cottar, each is a cog in the great and complex machine of feudal farming.

This village may still exist today, releasing a daily quota of accountants, secretaries, managers, council workers and members of a score of other trades and vocations, each person bound for a different and private niche in the workaday world. In the Domesday village, however, everybody knew everybody else's business. They had to do so, for the village was both the brain and the powerhouse of feudal farming. Every rule, custom and work practice had to be known by all, every work contract honoured, every obligation performed and every right enjoyed. Each manor had a code of practice of the utmost complexity and the villagers were locked into an intricate system of communal farming that promised them no more than the prospect of survival in all but the meanest years, when some at least could expect to perish.

In many regions and localities the movement into open-field farming

never arrived or was modest in its effects. In such places ancient countryside patterns endured. Here only the age-old commons were open and the land had a more secretive air. Moving through such countryside the view was restricted by the high banks and hedgerows bordering snaking trackways ground deep into the land through centuries of usage. Clambering up to spy through a hedgerow gap one might see a succession of small fields, each bounded by dense hedgerows packed with oak, cherry, field maple, ash, elm, hazel and crab apple. Some of these fields were inherited from Roman times, others were much older still. Periodically these hedgerows broaden to embrace a small wood, and with all its hedges and woodlands the country has an intimate and almost a forested aura. Though the trees and hedgerows obstruct the view it is plain that this is not village country, but hamlets and farmsteads are numerous. There are no vast open fields where one might walk across the clinging ploughsoil for a couple of miles without meeting an obstruction. Ridge and furrow cultivation has been introduced into several of the pre-existing fields without the campaigns of hedge removal and ditch-filling which accompanied its arrival in other areas. Some of these fields contain strips, but these are parcelled out not amongst a flock of village tenants but between a handful of peasants from a nearby hamlet or neighbouring farms. In scenic terms the countryside is delightfully patterned and diverse, reminiscent of

113

the enticing scenes depicted on old railway posters attracting travellers into Devon or the counties of the Welsh Marches.

In Domesday, large areas, mainly in the north of England, are recorded as being 'waste'. One must be careful with this word, for the commons were often referred to as 'waste' and yet they were indispensable sources of grazing, timber and fuel. However, the wastes which concern us here were associated with heavy falls in the value of estates between King Edward's reign and 1086. There is no mystery here, for these lands in Yorkshire, Durham and Lancashire (which was not covered in detail by the survey) bore the brunt of the Conqueror's terrible Harrying of the North in 1069–71. There were local insurrections in other parts of England and wasted estates were numerous in Cheshire, Derbyshire and the Welsh Marches. Exasperated by a succession of northern revolts, the Conqueror launched a campaign of genocide and destruction against his rebellious subjects. According to a contemporary account

The Norman conquerors extended their control in the English localities by building motte and bailey castles such as this. Domestic buildings often were built in the bailey, with a timber tower or keep often standing on the crown of the taller mound of the motte. Vana Haggerty/Macdonald & Co.

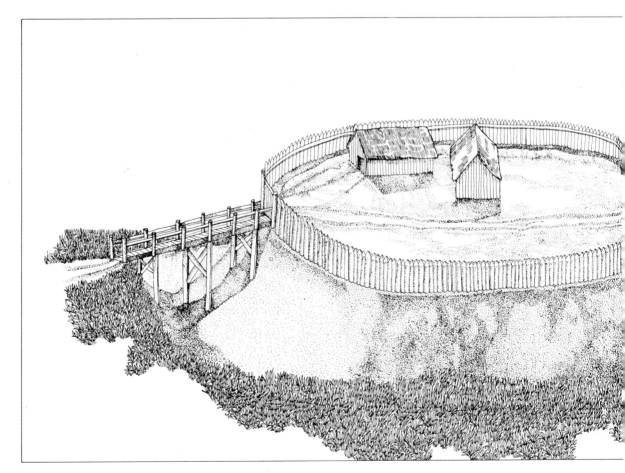

every kind of food he ordered to be heaped together and burned. The famine that had raged for a year was by such methods so aggravated, and so horrible was the misery, that the wretched survivors were compelled to subsist upon the flesh of horses, cats and even human flesh. During this time, it is said no less than 100,000 people perished. Appalling it was, in the silent houses, in the deserted streets and roads to see rotting corpses, covered with myriads of worms, in an atmosphere foul with the stench of putrefaction ... On the once frequented road from York to Durham as far as the eye could reach not a single inhabited village was to be seen.

The *Anglo-Saxon Chronicle* is more terse, telling us that in Yorkshire in 1069 the king 'laid waste all the shire'.

Domesday was compiled almost two decades after these vile events yet it reveals countrysides still maimed and barren from the carnage. Cheshire lay on the periphery of the slaughter and had 162 wasted estates in 1070 and only 102 which were intact; by 1086 there were still 58 estates in the

county which were wholly or partly crippled. So many of the Domesday entries for the north of England tell us little more or no more than *wasteas est*: it is waste.

We have much to learn about the appearance of Domesday English villages. Ironically it is the north of England, so patchily described in Domesday, that preserves most evidence of a type of Norman village. After the Harrying, countrysides often had to be built anew, with new feudal settlements created to house survivors brought in to revive and work the ravaged estates. Hundreds of such villages were planned. Dwellings were set in orderly rows along one or both sides of a through-road, often with a ribbon of green intervening between the houses and the roadside. Sometimes a triangle of green was bordered by roads and the roads lined with dwellings. Long narrow plots of equal length and of equal width ran back from the dwellings, providing land for horticulture or small livestock and terminating at a back lane. The essence of a planned Norman lay-out can still be recognised in hosts of surviving Northern villages. We do not know whether planned lay-outs were to be found amongst the older and enduring village forms and archaeology does not have a great deal to tell us about peasant dwellings of the Domesday period.

By this time it is likely that a form of dwelling known as the long-house had come into general use. This was a small, narrow, rectangular dwelling divided into two parts by a cross-passage which separated the single family living room from a byre where sheep or a milk cow were sheltered, all living under the same thatched roof using the same door and in close enough contact for the body heat of the animals to warm the peasant household. Excavations at the deserted hamlet of Gomeldon in Wiltshire revealed an early phase represented by a single dwelling of the twelfth century. This was a long house with rounded corners measuring only 25 feet by 14 feet (7.8 by 4.2 m). The poky living room was walled in flint and had a tiny adjoining timber outhouse with an oven and was screened from the timber-framed byre. Such dwellings were flimsy and short-lived, and early in the next century the house was demolished, its site becoming the yard for a pair of more substantial flint-walled long-houses. At the deserted village of Goltho in Lincolnshire excavation revealed a dwelling dating roughly to the time of Domesday. The rectangular house was built of a primitive form of timber-framing with unsquared timbers set in post holes forming the framework of the walls and providing the support for the roof.

Most of the Norman landowners lived in manor houses built larger but according to the same principles. Surviving timber-framed houses of the fourteenth, fifteenth and sixteenth centuries are quite numerous and so one might expect that somewhere in England a Norman timber-framed manor might survive. However, the life of a house was bound to be modest

so long as it was built upon posts set in the soil, for these timbers would quickly rot. Medieval building techniques evolved through several stages, with the ends of posts buried but set on flat stones; then set on flat stones standing upon the surface, and then jointed into horizontal 'sill beams' raised above the levels of damp and decay on low rubble or brick walls. It was the last-named technique which allowed the construction of timber-framed houses which could exist virtually indefinitely.

A small minority of Norman houses were built in stone and a few examples survive to this day. They included some rural manor houses and some town houses which are often associated with the old Jewish financial community. These dwellings were mainly of the type known as 'first-floor halls', with the great living-cum-reception room being built with an adjoining 'solar' or private sitting room at first-floor level above a vaulted undercroft or storage area and with the hall reached via an external stone staircase. The late-twelfth-century undercroft at Burton Agnes old hall near Bridlington provides the best-preserved example of an undercroft of the type described.

Domesday England was an expanse of working farmland of many different kinds. Towns were small but not insignificant and the land was

Norman domestic architecture at Burton Agnes old hall in Yorkshire. Norman stone halls usually had living accommodation at first floor level above a vaulted undercroft or storage area such as this. Richard Muir.

very largely peopled by peasants who were the targets of heavy exploitation and were socially divided into different grades. Depending upon the history and organisation of local farming these peasants might live together in small to medium-sized villages of insubstantial thatched dwellings or be dispersed around the countryside in hamlets and farmsteads. Wildlife was much more numerous and diverse than today; the beaver and bear were already extinct but both the wolf and the boar still roamed in the less disturbed habitats. Two of the commonest forms of English wildlife, the fallow deer and the rabbit, were both introduced and nurtured by the Normans.

Robin Hood's England

LIKE KING ARTHUR, ROBIN HOOD is a shadowy figure, a man who probably did exist but whose popular image has become so festooned with fanciful trappings as to bear little relationship to reality. He stands at the centre of many perceptions of the medieval world, and here we can explore the kinds of scenes and buildings which were commonplace in his time.

Certainly the notion that medieval England contained unbroken tracts of 'merrie Greenwood' in which an outlaw band could become lost to the world is false, but before exploring the countryside we must try to locate Robin Hood in time and space.

A detailed investigation of the Robin Hood legends has been accomplished by the historian, Professor J. C. Holt. First it is shown that the surname Robynhod, a peculiar name which must have derived from outlaw legends that were already current, had been adopted by 1296. Various men called Robert Hod or Robin Hood appear in medieval documents and it is hard to know which, if any, of them was the 'real' Robin Hood. Around 1400, or a little after, the current Robin Hood legends were combined in a long poem, 'A Gest of Robyn Hode'. Here the locale of the outlaw's camp is not Sherwood Forest, but Barnsdale, about 30 miles (50 km) further north and just south of Pontefract near the Great North Road. Barnsdale lay in the great manor of Wakefield, whose surviving court rolls provide much detailed information about the medieval countryside in the south of Yorkshire. Various Hoods lived on this manor but none of them can be positively linked to the outlaw. However, a Robert Hod or Hobbehod, who was a tenant of the archbishopric of York, was named as a fugitive in 1226. His home is not identified, but it could have been in the large manor of Sherburn-in-Elmet, not very far from Barnsdale. Whoever the real Robin Hood was, by the end of the century Robynhod was being adopted as a surname and during the fourteenth century the Robin Hood legends became widespread; in William Langland's *Piers Plowman* of about 1377 a character admits that he cannot remember the words of the paternoster, 'But I kan [know] rymes of Robynhod and Randolph, earl of Chester'. And so the real Robin Hood seems to have been a thirteenth-century outlaw operating in the Barnsdale area, a locality where the road to the north

bifurcated with one branch, now the A1, which headed towards Ferry-bridge capturing the traffic in the fourteenth century and the older Roman route going to Pontefract. The Barnsdale area was notorious for its bandits, so prominent travellers increased their escorts when passing this way.

Barnsdale did not lie in a forest but was between the royal hunting forests of Sherwood and Knaresborough. As the Robin Hood legends evolved they acquired a 'greenwood' garnish which reflected popular opposition to the Forest Law and the multiplication of private hunting reserves. At the time when Robert Hod was outlawed, forest covered at least one fifth of England. This was not woodland but legally designated forest and within the forest area as a whole, a quarter or less of the land was actually wooded. Some forests, like Dartmoor, were moorland while most included large areas of working farmland surrounding a wooded core. In Saxon times various royal hunting forests existed, in the core of the New Forest, in the upper Pennine dales, the Weald, Welsh Marches, Essex and elsewhere. After the conquest William established many new forests, and placed them under Forest Law which imposed harsh penalties on those who disturbed or injured the deer and woodland, whether as poachers or in

Fallow deer were introduced by the Normans and were the most sought-after beasts of the chase. Richard Muir.

the course of day-to-day farming operations. At the time of Domesday only twenty-five forests existed, more were created by William's successors or in the twelfth and early thirteenth centuries and the Forest Law was formalised and extended under Henry I and Henry II.

The area subject to the forest courts was at its most extensive under Henry II (1154–89) with over a quarter of the realm affected. There was great public opposition to the imposition of laws which allowed deer to feed on crops without disturbance and huntsmen to career across the plough-lands and pastures, and which required the maiming of all peasant dogs kept within the forest. By the time of Robert Hod the forest area was contracting, fines and impositions were becoming less severe, but Forest Law was still extremely unpopular and those who succeeded in thwarting the foresters could expect to become local heroes. Around the era of Robert Hod it was said of Alan de Neville, chief forester over all England's forests, that when monks sought his body for burial the king replied, 'I will have his wealth, you shall have the body, and the demons of hell his soul.' Alan seemed to have served his king too well. Some forests were in isolated backwaters of the realm, like Dartmoor, Exmoor, Lancashire and the North York Moors, but many were close to the agricultural heartlands and at the peak of the royal forest extensions one could ride quite directly from the Wash to the Hampshire basin without ever leaving a designated forest, or from Colchester to Dorset or Bristol to the Peak District without being outside a forest for very long. But to understand the thirteenth-century countryside one must remember that 'forest' was a legal concept and that even within the forests the wooded areas which provided the deer with their silent, shady retreats were far less extensive than the agricultural areas. Once introduced, the fallow deer proved far more readily adaptable and successful than the rabbits which the Normans also introduced, but they remained very valuable and there may actually be more fallow deer living in England today than in the days of Robin Hood.

Meanwhile, the forest provided the king with hunting and fresh venison and other game for the table. This was important, for the court was forever on the move from one royal manor to the next, so that the Plantagenet kings probably saw more of England than any previous monarchs or commoners. The forests yielded light and heavy timber with forest trees being coppiced and pollarded in the conventional manner; they provided pannage for pigs and often contained specialised cattle farms or 'vaccaries', horse stud farms, and produced revenues from rents and fines. However, there were considerable costs associated with the tending of the forest and the administration of Forest Law. Overseeing the forests, after the office of chief forester was divided in 1239, were two justices of the peace, in charge respectively of forests north and south of the River Trent. Each forest had its own warden and each warden had subordinate foresters, woodwards, agisters, regarders and verderers. The verderers were judges at the forest courts, woodwards protected the trees and timber, agisters controlled the grazing, regarders surveyed all aspects of the forest while each forester had responsibility for a distinct walk or bailiwick within the forest. Foresters and regarders were often knights and could claim special rights; for example, Sir John de Davenport, chief forester for Leek and Macclesfield in the early fourteenth century, claimed two shillings and a salmon for every robber chief captured and a shilling for each member of his band. Some hermits lived in the solitude of the forest woodland and were well placed to report on the deer and their poachers.

Although some great nobles and churchmen hunted extensive chases not subject to Forest Law, the forests were royal hunting reserves. Most nobles of substance sought to obtain deer parks, which were much smaller than forests and which served as protected reserves from which the game could be released and hunted across the neighbouring countrysides. The typical deer park had an area of around 150 to 200 acres (60 to 80 ha) and boundaries protected by great earthen banks and ditches, hedges and palings. Some parks were created in Saxon times but it was only after the conquest that they became common features of the countryside and after 1200 that every noble landlord had, or wished to have, one, the Dukes of Cornwall owning 29 parks and the Earls of Lancaster, 45. At their peak of popularity, around 1300, England may have contained more than 3000 parks with a fiftieth of the total area being devoted to this form of land use. Most deer parks were created in the existing demesne woodland of an estate, with massive amounts of peasant labour being conscripted to build the protective earthworks and palings. A few deer parks were established

Hunting fallow deer with bow and arrows from a fourteenth-century manuscript illustration. Here a latter day 'Maid Marion' is depicted; archery was popular amongst women as well as men. The British Library.

on land seized unlawfully from peasant holdings and commons. Robert Hod lived at a time when deer parks were proliferating and when, like the forests, they were targets for popular complaint and magnets for poachers.

We have seen that the Domesday countryside was largely working farmland. During the two centuries which followed population increased considerably and may actually have doubled. This growth put enormous pressure on the resources of the countryside and upon the remaining areas of woodland and waste. Henry II, hyperactive both at work and at play, was the greatest of the hunting monarchs. It was said that 'He was addicted to the chase beyond measure; at the crack of dawn he was off on horseback, traversing waste lands, penetrating forests and climbing the mountain tops, and so he passed his restless days'. In the reigns that followed the royal perception of the forests gradually changed. Some were still hunted, but increasingly it was the rent and sale of forest assets which were regarded as the main sources of value.

An archery contest in the mid-fourteenth century from the Luttrell Psalter. Interestingly the archer who has just scored the bulls-eye wears a hood, causing one to wonder whether he represents Robin Hood. The British Library.

King John, forever short of funds, received 700 pounds weight of silver from the nobles and free tenants of the Honour of Lancaster for allowing them the right to cultivate forest land free from interference from the king's bailiffs, and three clauses in the Magna Carta of 1215 lightened the burden of Forest Law on the barons. In 1217 King Henry III was pressurised into issuing a new Forest Charter which disafforested some

areas and tempered the law in others. Much royal forest remained and periodically forest tenants would be exploited through the imposition of special taxes or the sale of concessions. In 1353 rioting followed a meeting of the forest court at Chester which culminated in 125 fines being imposed by the Chief Forester of Wirral. The Black Prince needed funds to support the French Wars.

As villages grew and new villages, hamlets and farmsteads were established much of the new farmland needed was obtained by 'assarting' or clearing the woodlands and colonising the waste. The ploughland was increased by establishing new open-field systems, by adding third, fourth or fifth fields to existing systems and by adding new furlongs to existing fields, while pastures and meadows might be won by clearing or draining the waste. Whether or not the local communities were aware of the fact, the English were becoming engaged in a grim race for survival, for whenever population growth outstripped the expansion of farming then famine would surely follow. Perhaps people were too busy with the day-to-day rituals of farming to ponder on what would happen when the resources of the waste ran out.

Sometimes great landowners initiated campaigns of assarting, sometimes whole village communities worked together to reduce a wood, but most frequently assarting was carried out piecemeal by individuals or by a few families. The assarted land could be assimilated into the communal open fields but most of the clearances seem to have been accomplished by free peasants who became the tenants of small hedged fields which were the fruits of their hard labours. In the areas of open-field farming such little irregular enclosures with their fringing hedgerows were commonly seen filling a zone between the established pastures and open ploughlands and the retreating woodland, wood pasture and rough grazings of the common waste. In the areas of ancient and more marginal countryside the assarts grew to fill large sections of the countryside with patchwork field patterns. In places which had considerable extents of Domesday woodland, like the forest of Arden in Warwickshire, whole landscapes could be transformed, with the woods becoming fieldscapes patterned by new hamlets, farmsteads and the moated homesteads of the most successful of assarters.

Robin Hood's England had many of the features of a modern third-world state: a population in which impoverished and exploited peasants greatly outnumbered members of all other classes; an overbearing land-owning class; a government which lacked the resources and capability to undertake national programmes of improvement, and population growth which was outstripping the capacity of the environment to satisfy the demands placed upon it. Given the unavoidable rise in population the

assarting movement was inevitable, whether it proceeded through legal or illegal channels. In areas like Arden where there was still ample scope for woodland clearance, parish populations could increase fourfold or even eightfold in the two centuries after Domesday. Assarted land yielded rents of around 2*d* (1.2p) per acre while well-managed woodland could be more profitable. Where the royal forests were concerned the position of the kings was difficult. Efforts could be made to prevent agricultural inroads, but these restrictions were extremely unpopular. At the same time, the sale of licences to assart produced welcome income, as did the levying of fines on those who had made illegal assarts. Many of the fines imposed by the medieval kings were more like rents and taxes than penalties. In 1204, for example, the men of Devon paid the crown 5000 marks for the dis-afforestation of the county, excluding Dartmoor.

Royal forest and manorial woodlands were by no means the only areas to be changed by the insatiable demand for farmland. The Domesday wood pastures were rapidly retreating under the pressure of grazing which prevented the establishment of new saplings. The open commons were also contracting as the making of 'intakes' of enclosed and privatised lands from their margins reduced the communal grazings. Under the Statute of Merton of 1250 lords were allowed to enclose common land providing that their tenants had ample pasture left – and the lord's interpretation of 'ample' might well be different from that of his vassals. Peasants and yeomen were also keen to enclose morsels of the common and would do so whenever the interests of the broader community were not jealously guarded.

The wetlands of England offered considerable scope for reclamation work. From times immemorial they had provided fish and wildfowl and their moist grazings were shared or 'intercommoned' by the communities living around their margins. In the centuries after Domesday the broad frontiers of shared land narrowed and then vanished as each village pressed its claims. Sodden pastures were transformed into hay meadows, the extra supplies of fodder allowing more livestock to be kept through the barren months of winter. Meadow land was usually more valuable than ploughland and its productivity was actually greater in areas, like the Somerset Levels, where the ground was inundated by spring floods. In areas like the Fens, where there was less likelihood of flooding, the conversion of fenland into ploughland was possible.

The most spectacular advances were made in the Fens surrounding the Wash and in the two and a half centuries following Domesday one of the poorer environments in England was converted into one of the richest, studded with plump villages and splendid churches. By building groynes, seabanks and dykes it was possible to advance the coastline and to drain the

Opposite: hermits living deep in the forest sometimes informed forest officials on the movement of deer and the activities of poachers. Note the wattle fence surrounding the hermitage.

inland fens protected by the seabanks and floodwater sluices. Historian Michael Williams estimates that

Opposite: *in this scene of a boarhunt, painted by Simon Benninck in the early sixteenth century to represent a December scene, we see typical managed medieval woodland. The woodland has a coppiced underwood, recently cut, in the foreground with oak and elm standards growing tall to produce heavier timber. The British Library.*

> between about 1150 and 1300 the ordinary men of the villages around the Wash engaged in a massive feat of reclamation that won some 16 square miles (41km²) from the marshland bordering the Wash and some 90 square miles (233 km²) from the fenland. The reclaimed land was used mainly for arable farming to feed what seemed to be a rapidly growing population. The evidence of their bustling youthfulness and energy in colonisation of the waste is etched indelibly on the landscape by a series of walls and dykes, and also by many additions, each dyke marking a step in the reclamation process.

Few wetlands stayed unaffected by the national appetite for farmland. Romney Marsh, the Somerset Levels, river floodplains around the Thames, Yorkshire Ouse and Humber and estuarine mudflats all shrank as the banks and ditches advanced. Areas noted for their harvests of eels, pike and mallard now yielded wheat, barley and hay.

The colonisers of the waste came in many guises: the solitary freeman with his axe and hedging tools; bands of villagers; confederations of village bands advancing like armies with spades and mattocks; forces of lay brethren despatched from monasteries; the tenants of abbots and those of the church militant, the Knights Templar. In the Lincoln Heath parish of Temple Bruer, north of Sleaford, the reclamation of the thinly populated heathlands was masterminded from a 'preceptory' or local headquarters of the crusading order established here around 1150 and now marked by ruins and the place-name Temple Farm.

In the north of England there were great opportunities for reclamation of lands ravaged and depopulated by the Harrying. The colonisation was initiated by both lay and ecclesiastical landlords, but it was the monastic communities who created the most distinctive countrysides. The early flowering of English monasticism under the regional Saxon monarchs was checked by the Viking raids and almost perished as the invaders looted one foundation after another. Following the Conquest, various continental orders were encouraged to establish houses in the Norman realm. Several orders participated in the great colonisation movement but the outstanding contribution was made by the Cistercians, partly because their rule required settlement in neglected backwaters which were insulated from the evils of the everyday world. Contrary to popular belief, the drive to colonise and maintain the expanding Cistercian estates was not spearheaded by the monks, who were expected to be concerned with higher matters, but by members of the large colonies of lay brothers established in each foundation. As grants and endowments rewarded communities with lands further and further from the abbey headquarters the Cistercians adopted the grange system of dispersed farms. The grange was a collection of farm buildings and a chapel managed by lay brothers but sometimes worked by peasant tenants. The attached land-holding was large, averaging around 500 acres (200 ha), while subordinate lodges often accommodated a few specialist farmworkers within the territory of the grange. The Cistercians established around 350 granges in England, almost three quarters of which lay to the north of the Severn and Wash. Williams estimates that Yorkshire alone supported 120 granges, at least three quarters of which were founded in the days of dramatic Cistercian expansion prior to 1200, with more than 40 per cent of these granges occupying land wasted during the Harrying of the North. Fountains Abbey, with no less than 26 granges, had the grandest monastic empire, while Byland, Jervaulx, Kirkstall, Rievaulx and Salley abbeys each had ten or more granges. Some of these granges were established in neglected backwaters, but in many cases monastic and peasant colonisation met head to head and almost always it was the evicted peasant who was the loser.

The Cistercian advance stimulated the eager continental demand for English wool. With their seemingly boundless estates the northern monasteries had a special advantage, being able to move their flocks from one walk or grazing to another, thus preventing the contamination of the pasture by pests and parasites. Monastic farming was not solely concerned with the wool trade. As well as the open upland and moorland sheep ranges the estates also included sheltered valley pastures and meadows and lowland arable holdings as well as hunting reserves in the Dales and marshland pastures and meadows near the coast.

At Roystone Grange in Derbyshire the landscape evolved from the one we explored in Roman times. At the end of the twelfth century the waste here was granted by Robert de Herthill to the Cistercian abbey at Garendon in Leicestershire. Work by M. Wildgoose shows that a grange with outbuildings was erected at the centre of five walled paddocks. The paddocks probably supplied the farmstead with arable crops, the vast 450-acre (182-ha) grazings beyond being enclosed within a perimeter wall and used to pasture a monastic flock of several hundred sheep. Gaps or 'sheep creeps' in the boundary wall gave access to the open land beyond. As the demand for wool gradually decreased in the thirteenth and fourteenth centuries the farm diversified, increasing its arable holding and converting an earlier building into a cowshed and dairy. Late in the fifteenth century this grange, like so many others, was let to private tenants and developed as a mixed farm. Our illustration shows the grange as it appeared in the mid-thirteenth century with ploughing in progress in one of the paddocks and with repairs being made to the medieval walls built

just one boulder thick with smaller stones placed upon the heaviest boulders of the wall base.

The post-Domesday expansion involved much more than the establishment of granges and new villages. In the uplands and in areas of ancient countryside it was also associated with the founding of thousands of solitary farmsteads. Professor W. G. Hoskins calculates that of the 15,000 farms in Devon, one fifth already existed in 1086 and that the majority of the remainder were established by 1350 as part of a great colonisation movement which reached its peak in the thirteenth century. Many of the farmsteads established by the greater free men and lesser nobles were moated homesteads with the dwelling and its principal outbuildings being surrounded by a rectangular moat. More than 5000 moated manors and farmsteads have been discovered in England and Wales. They range in age from the middle of the twelfth century to the end of the fifteenth century, with the peak period of moat-making being in the thirteenth century. The moats served an array of functions, providing a reserve of water to quench fires in the timber-framed buildings within, helping to provide a supply of fish, serving as status symbols which echoed the moats of the grander castles and sometimes providing protection against pests and sneak thieves.

Robin Hood lived in an age of great commercial vitality when new towns emerged, old ones expanded and village markets proliferated. During the

Simon Manby's reconstruction of the grange of Garendon Abbey at Roystone Grange as it existed in the mid-thirteenth century. Note the men engaged in drystone walling.

131

thirteenth century around 3000 new markets were authorised, most of them the results of initiatives by their manorial lords, who hoped to profit from market tolls after securing the necessary market charter. Usually this charter permitted a market to be held on a specified day of the week and traders could organise their affairs in order to circulate from one local market to the next. Many of the new markets were short-lived and most were humdrum little gatherings with the more exciting, expensive and exotic goods only being available at the great annual fairs staged by members of the elite of trading centres. The rigidly feudal nature of rural society restricted opportunities for aspiring merchants and entrepreneurs and the growing towns began to exist as islands of enterprise. Any urban community of substance sought to secure its freedom to govern its own affairs and destiny, and this freedom could usually be bought in the costly form of a royal charter which granted the right of self-government and regulation to the new borough. In 1200, for example, the burgesses of Ipswich, then a bustling trading and fishing port with around 3000 inhabitants, secured a charter from King John which granted self-government in return for an annual rent of £65. At this time London, York and Norwich were the greatest cities of the realm with populations of more

Robin Hood would have been familiar with timber-framed manor houses such as this one, which stood at Wintringham in Huntingdonshire in the thirteenth century. The posts are set on padstones to give a certain protection against decay. Based on work by the archaeologist G. Beresford.
Helen Clarke & Peter Leach: The Archaeology of Medieval England.

than 20,000 and the hierarchy of towns extended downwards through major provincial centres like Exeter and Bristol to country towns like Stafford with populations of less than 5000. As the towns grew building plots were subdivided, with each trader anxious to secure a trading frontage, no matter how narrow, on a busy thoroughfare. The congestion of timber-framed buildings which resulted heightened the risks of disastrous fires, but although some of the wealthier burgesses responded by building in stone, most houses in towns were of timber, wattle and thatch.

Stone was a bulky and expensive commodity, but much in demand because of the remarkable church- and castle-building campaigns which took place in the twelfth and thirteenth centuries. Taking a sample of 85 cathedrals and abbeys, Richard Morris found that between 1175 and 1250 these churches alone experienced some 75 major new building campaigns. In June of 1253 works at Westminster Abbey were providing employment for no less than 426 tradesmen and labourers. The realm is said to have been awash with silver and a fine heritage of castles and of churches, cathedrals and abbeys in the Early English and Decorated styles survives to remind us of the vigour and vibrancy of thirteenth-century England.

In the previous chapter we saw how Domesday England was a place of old countryside and working countrysides. As populations increased in the years that followed, the agricultural effort was shifted into a higher gear as attempts were made to sustain a surging population. This surge was accompanied by an intensification of feudal impositions on the peasantry, with the abundance and cheapness of labour encouraging landlords to exploit their vassals. For those who could escape the bondage of the manor the town shone out as a beacon of opportunity and the great building works offered employment to the skilled and unskilled alike.

It would be very difficult to reconstruct a particular countryside from the evidence contained in Domesday Book but the availability of medieval documents ranging from the records of manor courts to royal charters and licences does allow at least a sketchy reconstruction of the appearance of many countrysides at the turn of the thirteenth century. Were I able to walk the couple of miles from the village of Ripley in Yorkshire to my home in the early years of the fourteenth century I would see many characteristic features of the medieval countryside. Leaving the village destined to gain its market and fair charter in 1357, I would skirt the northern edge of the lord's deer park following a road shared by monks and laymen and cross the bounds of the Forest of Knaresborough. Turning southwards on a track which ascends the ridge overlooking the valley of the Nidd I gain a fine impression of the diversity of the medieval countryside. I stand in a salient of the royal forest which juts north of the river at this point. To the south is the manor of Ripley, then as now in the hands of the Ingilby family.

Northward lies the territory of Brimham, controlled by Fountains Abbey and worked from a grange, while in the distance beyond are the heathland grazings controlled by Byland Abbey. All the land to the west lies in the Forest of Knaresborough but the woodland is broken by ploughlands, pastures and commons. Close to the trackside there is assarting in progress with about 30 acres (12 ha) of woodland being cleared while the ring of more distant axes can be heard in woods just across the river. A swathe of common meadow land follows the floodplain of the river, and just beyond lies the village of Hampsthwaite, currently being reorganised to accommodate a triangular market green following the creation by Edward I of a Friday Market and three-day fair on his estates here in 1304. The track takes me through the little village of Clint, its peasants, weavers and spur-makers living in hovels with a tavern and (probably) a moated manor near by.

In the centuries to come this little forest village is destined to become virtually deserted, but records which survive of a sordid and tragic incident which occurred here in 1325 show how clues to the appearance of vanished scenes and places can be gleaned from unlikely sources – in this case records of the court of the Liberty of Knaresborough.

On the Sunday after Epiphany, William, a villager of Clint, quarrelled in his local tavern with William del Ridding (his name means William of the assart). William Clint left the tavern, pursued by del Ridding, who was armed with bow and arrows. He sought refuge in the house of villager Agnes Serveys, and as del Ridding broke down the front door, Clint fled out the back. This suggests that the dwelling was of the long-house type, with a cross passage running between the front and back doors and separating the living room and byre. He was pursued across several hedges towards the head of the village as arrows whistled by. From this information it seems that each village dwelling had a long hedged plot or 'toft' attached, so that Clint had to jump a succession of hedges to reach the top of the village. The chase continued for two more miles until Clint fell exhausted and was killed.

CHAPTER ELEVEN

The Tortured Realm of Pilgrims and Piers Plowman

BY THE FOURTEENTH CENTURY THE English language had evolved to a point where it would be roughly, though far from completely, comprehensible to the people of modern England. The century saw the emergence of two of the most important contributors to our literature, Geoffrey Chaucer (*c.* 1340–1400) and William Langland (*c.*1330–*c.*1386). Neither of these poets set out to describe familiar countrysides for their own sake although through their work one can obtain glimpses of delightful settings which gave pleasure to those who could enjoy them. Both poets also lived through what was probably the most ghastly phase in the history of our nation – the first violent eruptions of the Black Death – although Chaucer gives only an oblique mention of the tragedy in which both his uncle and grandfather probably died, perhaps considering it too frightful to describe and possibly fearful that the mere mention of the disease could bring about infection.

A notion of the comprehensibility of fourteenth-century English can be gained from the Prologue of Langland's great work *The Vision of Piers Plowman*:

> Ac [But] on a May morwenynge on Malverne hilles
> Me Bifel a ferly [wonder], of Fairye me thoghte.
> I was wery forwandred and wente me to rest
> Under a brood bank by a bourne syde;
> And as I lay and lenede and loked on the watres
> I slombred into a slepying, it sweyed so murye
> [sounded so sweetly].

Although these words capture some of the enchantment of the English countryside they are not a celebration of the national territory. Nationalism was still a largely meaningless concept and would remain so until Elizabethan times, when Shakespeare would express the growing national sentiments of his own day through the lips of his historical kings. In the

days of Langland and Chaucer the appreciation of the delights of the countryside was well entrenched but loyalty was owed to feudal superiors and not to the land and its people.

Langland is a largely mysterious figure. He seems to have come from the Malvern locality and may have been educated at Oxford before moving to London. He was neither wealthy nor privileged and seems at times to have existed as an itinerant, surviving by reciting prayers and verses. While supporting the established social order he satirised the injustices of the fourteenth-century society and stressed the importance of justice and charity to the quest for Christian perfection. Chaucer, in contrast, was a prominent diplomat and courtier. In comparison to Langland he was more of a storyteller and less of a moralist.

In Chaucer's *The Canterbury Tales* a pilgrimage to the shrine of St Thomas à Becket at Canterbury unites a band of people of different background and character. To pass the time each pilgrim in turn adopts the role of storyteller so that the work provides us with a passport to the fourteenth-century world of the courtly knight, the plump prioress, the friar who was skilled in the art of begging, the rascally miller and their companions. The Wife of Bath was a seasoned traveller of many pilgrimages and these expeditions provided her with the opportunities for companionship and merriment, while for many of her poor compatriots the pilgrimage was not only a religious experience but a relief from the repetitive drudgery of day-to-day life.

The network of rutted roads and dusty lanes which the pilgrims plied were unequal to the demands of the day. The main arterial system was largely inherited from Roman times but was far less well maintained than it had been a thousand years previously. Over time morsels of new routeway had developed along with the rising market towns and villages which they served, but the problem of bad communications was virtually universal. Within London there were a few stretches of paved streets, though most of the major provincial cities had their thoroughfares unpaved until the fifteenth or sixteenth centuries. In winter many highways became impassable and even in summer wheeled transport was seriously disadvantaged. The affluent pilgrim or traveller would prefer to ride on horseback or travel in a wheel-less litter slung between two horses harnessed fore and aft. Meanwhile the commerce of the realm moved by narrow river barges or was carried in panniers slung on the sides of pack horses. Occasionally, in desperation, a wealthy landowner or the aldermen of a borough would rebuild a bridge or spread rubble on a rutted highway, but more frequently

Servile peasants reaping and stooking grain for their domineering lord. After the Black Death such scenes became less common. From Holinshed's Chronicles of England. The Treasurer and Masters of the Bench of Lincoln's Inn.

narrow parochialism would argue against improvements whose benefits would be enjoyed, in part, by strangers.

The opening of Parliament was postponed in 1339 because most of its members were unable to get to London. In addition to the problems of the roads was that of robbery or worse. This threat increased during the fourteenth century and in 1348 the Commons noted that: 'throughout all the shires of England, robbers, thieves and other malefactors, both on foot and on horseback ride the highways in diverse places'. In consequence Chaucer's pilgrims travelled in a body accompanied by an armed knight.

Some domestic buildings of substance survive from the days of Langland and Chaucer, Stokesay Castle, one of the most evocative and well-preserved of these, being around a century old at the time of the *Canterbury Tales*. The great majority of people were peasants occupying hovels that would become derelict and in need of rebuilding within their own lifetimes. In *Piers Plowman*, Langland tells of a wretched housewife struggling to raise her large family and perform her chores all within a single room. Chaucer in the *Nun's Priest's Tale* describes the 'poor widow

Chaucer and Langland would have been familiar with dwellings like this. It was reconstructed at the Weald and Downland museum, Singleton, West Sussex, by members of Brighton and Hove Archaeological Society and based on evidence from the excavation of a deserted village at Hangleton which was deserted in the fourteenth century. Note the smoke hole in the gable of the roof. Richard Muir.

somewhat advanced in age' who dwelled in a 'narrow cottage' with her two daughters, three large sows and a sheep called Malle:

> Full sooty was her bower, and likewise her hall,
> In which she ate full many a slender meal.

Now able to draw on the insights of medieval archaeology we can more easily imagine the sort of dwellings which Langland and Chaucer described and knew so well. The most typical peasant homestead of the fourteenth century was still a long-house, a narrow single-storeyed thatched building crudely partitioned to provide adjacent quarters, one room for the peasant household and a byre for their livestock. The narrow cottage mentioned by Chaucer was similarly both home and byre, but since it seems to have boasted a hall or living room and a bower or bedroom it was a mite more spacious than the run-of-the-mill hovels with just the one domestic room, as mentioned by Langland. The hall and bower were sooty because the cottage lacked any chimney, the smoke from the open hearth, which would have burned in the centre of the living room, hanging heavily in the air until it seeped away through a smoke hole in the thatch. Not until Elizabethan times in the more affluent south or the seventeenth or eighteenth centuries in the north and west would the rural poor be able to aspire to anything more durable or comfortable than a hovel such as this.

Langland and Chaucer were born at a time of severe rural overpopulation. The Domesday population of England had roughly doubled to reach a level of around five million and the signs of land hunger were already etched upon the countryside. By the start of the fourteenth century economic difficulties began to be experienced and the effects of a distinct deterioration in the climate intensified the pressures on an over-worked landscape. These dismal tendencies formed the background to a calamity of almost unimaginable proportions. If England was a place of gloom and forebodings, the gloom would have lifted in 1346 with the victories over the French at Crecy and over the Scots at Neville's Cross. Informed sources then became aware of a great plague which was advancing westwards across continental Europe.

Epidemics of various kinds were part and parcel of medieval life, affecting both mankind and livestock, particularly when populations were weakened by famine or their flocks by fodder shortages and waterlogging rains, which were becoming heavier and more frequent. This, however, was a plague of unprecedented virulence. It gained footholds in Hampshire and Dorset in the autumn of 1348 and by the following autumn it had killed more than 5000 citizens in London alone.

The Black Death originated in the vicinity of Peking in 1333 and moved

The Black Death devastated the whole of Europe. This contemporary illustration shows the burial of plague victims at Tournai in 1349. Bibliothèque Royale Albert, Belgium.

westwards by land along the silk roads and by sea to India and then along the Muslim pilgrim routes to Mecca. Spread along the trade routes by the black rat, host to the flea which carried the disease, it arrived in the Crimea in 1346 and there it was deliberately introduced into a Genoese trading post via infected corpses cast over the walls. In flight to Messina in Sicily, the Genoese brought the Black Death to Europe and it entered England via Melcombe in Dorset.

This may not have been the first visit of this vile plague to our shores. Possibly a previous eruption was responsible for the wholesale decline of population following the collapse of Roman rule, while Bede described an epidemic which had depopulated the southern shores of Britain and 'destroyed great multitudes of men' in his native Northumbria in 664. Thereafter each century witnessed one or more devastating outbreaks of disease; typhus, typhoid and dysentery being the culprits which most frequently assailed populations already weakened by famine. A particularly severe famine afflicted most of Europe in 1315–17 and was accompanied by the inevitable onslaught of plague. The chronicler, William of Newburgh, provided a chilling account of an earlier plague which had assailed the country in 1196:

> After the crowds of poor had been dying on all sides of want, a most savage plague ensued, as if from air corrupted by the dead bodies of the poor . . . Day after day it seized so many and finished off so many more that there was scarcely to be found any to give heed to the sick or to bury the dead. After it had raged on all sides for five or six months, it subsided when the winter cold came.

By 1349 the new plague had reached Scotland and Wales and all of England was in its grip. More than one third of the population perished and there can have been scarcely a single survivor that had not lost close relatives and friends. Although many people can still name 1348 as the year of the arrival of the Black Death fewer realise that it returned again and again; 1361, 1369, 1371, 1379 and 1390 experienced epidemics of particular severity and the seventeenth century was well advanced before people could feel at all secure from infection. There were outbreaks in 1603 and 1625 and a terrifying epidemic in 1665. When the civilised world believed that the disease was passing away into the realms of history Bombay was stricken in 1896, the actual causes of the pestilence having only been identified two years previously when an outbreak occurred in Hong Kong.

The epidemics of 1348 and 1361 affected town and country alike, although in the course of time the Black Death increasingly became a scourge of the filthy and congested cities. Refugees would flee in droves from affected towns and were unwelcome in the rural areas to which they resorted to evade infection. However, the effects of the disease were more lasting and profound in the countryside. In England, as in most of Europe, the supply of potential farmland was running out. As population grew the land area had to support more peasants and as the climate worsened yields became poorer and less reliable. Increasingly desperate efforts to maintain or raise production only accelerated the exhaustion of the soil. Throughout Europe population retreated from the hills and marginal farmlands. In Iceland there was a traumatic switch from farming to fishing and in England hill farms were abandoned, vineyards were grubbed up and farming in the sodden clay vales favoured cattle rearing following repeated failures of the grain crops.

Before the pestilence struck labour was cheap and over-abundant. The gulf between the classes in feudal society widened as landlords increased the burden of obligations and landless families sank into the depths of destitution. Within a few seasons, however, the economic situation in the countryside was transformed. Following the great mortality estate after estate lacked tenants to work the land. Peasants who had previously accepted the most onerous obligations swiftly realised that their labour had become a scarce and valuable resource. They could press for greatly improved conditions and if their demands were refused then they might slip away illegally in the night to take up a vacant holding on another depopulated estate where the terms were favourable and no questions would be asked. There was already a tendency for the more affluent peasants to purchase their freedom from their landlords, the cash which accrued then being used to hire wage-earning labourers. Such labour now became expensive and landlords confronted by restless and fractious feudal tenants and increasingly expensive hired labour cast around for alternative means of farming their estates.

In the twelfth century England had begun to enjoy an agricultural trading boom in which wool was the leading export commodity. Early in the fourteenth century the trade slumped as part of a general European economic decline. Then London-based Merchant Adventurer companies discovered a continental market for English cloth, it being much more economical for customers to purchase the manufactured cloth than to import wool that bore a heavy burden of export duties. This trade blossomed when the Adventurers by-passed the town-based weaving guilds with their costly restrictions and encouraged the development of rural cottage-based spinning, weaving, fulling and dyeing industries.

Feudal landlords responded to the situation in different ways, traces of which are frequently still displayed in the countryside. Some allowed

Medieval sheep were smaller and more wiry than most modern breeds. This flock was carved on a bench at Altarnun in Cornwall in the early sixteenth century. Richard Muir.

farming to proceed in the traditional manner, hoping that vacant tenancies would eventually be filled or encouraging immigration by leasing demesne or open-field land at low rents. Others cashed in on the buoyant demand for wool by grassing over the demesne and empty holdings and raising sheep (or cattle). Others still sought to remove rather than fortify the weakened village communities or to rid themselves of undisciplined or less economic peasants by wholesale evictions, followed by the conversion of the ploughlands and commons into what were, in effect, sheep ranches.

The new outlooks caused many voids to appear on the map of village England. Previous centuries had witnessed the multiplication of villages and hamlets as the need for land spawned settlements in every vacant niche of the countryside. The fourteenth century was the only century during the last millennium in which the population of England – and that of the world also – did not increase, but declined. Although the population began to grow again in the fifteenth century the evictions continued and dispossessed tenants starved at the roadside or migrated to fill the gaps which the Black Death was still carving in the towns. We still do not know how many English villages perished on the altar of the golden fleece but they would probably number a few thousand rather than a few hundred. When he died, in 1491, John Rous, a chantry priest of Warwick, left behind the unpublished manuscript of a History of England in which he listed some

Iron shears such as these were used until quite recent times. Note the representation of the farm dwellings in the background. The British Library (c. 1560).

fifty-eight depopulated villages, all lying within just a dozen miles of Warwick. He did not know the nationwide pattern of destruction but speculated that: 'If such destruction as that in Warwickshire took place in other parts of the country it would be a national danger.' In fact, in several parts of the East Midlands and north-eastern England the destruction was no less severe.

The cruel evictions continued through the Tudor era and the controversy surfaced in Sir Thomas More's *Utopia* of 1515:

> Look in what parts of the realm doth grow the finest and therefore dearest wool, there noblemen and gentlemen: yea, and certain Abbots . . . leave no ground for tillage, they enclose all into pasture: they throw down houses: they pluck down towns [villages] and leave nothing standing but only the church to be made a sheepcote.

In any particular place the survival of peasant tillage or the creation of an estate of large hedged sheep pastures peopled by few but shepherds depended on local circumstances and the attitudes of the land-owning dynasty. With the slow decay of feudalism, the reduction of the influence of the church and the rise of entrepreneurship there arose an influential class of hard-faced and calculating men whose like abound in the Britain of the 1980s. The old feudalism had advanced exploitation to the limits of human endurance and cast the villein or bordar as a mere chattel of his lord. But at least it recognised a bond of dependency between each rank in society.

All this is not to say that the feudal countryside of the open ploughland and common would have endured unchanged had the Black Death not intervened. Men of ambition were as frequently found among the peasant classes as among those of the entrepreneurs of the emerging middle class and the land-owning aristocracy. Before the Black Death when open-field farming was still advancing in some areas its gradual dismantlement was beginning in others. The ambitious bondsman strove to buy his freedom. Both bondsman and freeman would grasp at every opportunity to enlarge their holdings and to improve the efficiency and productivity of their efforts. Sometimes this involved them in assarting or the enclosure of common land, the legality of which was dubious. Often sheer greed undermined the communal ideal and Langland described the greedy peasant who sought to enlarge his strip by ploughing into the edge of that of his neighbour: 'If I went to the plough I pinched so narrowly that I would steal a foot of land or a furrow.' Frequently, however, changes were sanctioned by agreement between the leading village tenants. Travel between dozens of scattered strips was wasteful of time and energy while conformity to the common rotation practised on the field or the furlong stifled initiative. In many estates and parishes the communal farming pattern which had existed in Robin Hood's day was gradually being transformed via a host of tiny changes. Peasants periodically agreed to exchanges of strips which allowed each to control more consolidated blocks of strips so that the old, regular patterns of division became obscured. By the close of the Middle Ages the erratic and piecemeal process of 'enclosure by agreement' had obliterated the outlines of communal farming in some parishes.

The communal and the entrepreneurial forms of peasant farming often existed as uncomfortable bedfellows. The agreements concerning piecemeal enclosure frequently required that after cropping the enclosed land be thrown open to grazing by the village herd, and at such times disputes between communal and individual rights were likely to be rife. Meanwhile the depopulation of villages and attempts by landlords to exclude peasant livestock from the age-old commons fuelled grievances which erupted into several full-scale peasant revolts during the century following the first outbreak of the Black Death.

Langland and Chaucer remind us that medieval people were not two-dimensional stereotypes but characters with all our own virtues, vices and concerns about morality. The realm through which they moved was quite diverse, for not only did the old distinction between ancient and champion or open-field countryside live on, but the champion countryside had become more varied. Seen from on high the patchwork of fallow field and ploughland was periodically broken by expanses of grassland where an estate had witnessed eviction and conversion to sheep or cattle pasture. Meanwhile the countrysides of communal cultivation were becoming less uniform as strips were consolidated, enclosed and taken out of the traditional farming system.

Although the 'merrie England' of Robin Hood's day was not as merry as some imagine, late fourteenth-century England was beset by environmental ills, disease and social turmoil. It was a sad and perilous place and during the century that followed society became obsessed with visions of mortality and decay. The Middle Ages gradually died in an atmosphere permeated by thoughts of death, with few glimmers of the exuberance of the Elizabethan era to come.

CHAPTER TWELVE

The Elizabethan Countryside Revealed

OUR IMAGES OF THE MEDIEVAL countryside are blurred. Historical documents, illustrations and paintings allow us to recognise patterns and tendencies, yet detailed views of particular places are lacking. What we need, of course, are contemporary large-scale maps – but the Middle Ages had run its course before such documents materialised. The oldest surviving map of any quality dates from 1444 and shows the village and fields of Boarstall in Buckinghamshire. However, at this time cartographers had still to come to terms with their craft: scale is greatly distorted and the use of symbols is crude and uncertain. During the following decades techniques of surveying and cartography were gradually refined, so that in the latter part of the reign of Elizabeth I (1558–1603) the leading landowners became able to commission maps of their estates which were of high quality.

Suddenly our appreciations of the old countrysides are transformed, as though a great bank of mist has lifted. Now we can see the size and shape of every field, sometimes the name of each field, the networks of roads and trackways, the positions of all the houses – and much more besides. When we compare such estate maps with modern large-scale maps, we can appreciate the remarkable changes which have taken place during the last three to four centuries. In many places the Elizabethan countryside has been virtually obliterated, although in others we can see how venerable features still form the framework of the scene. Sometimes it is apparent that the Elizabethan countryside contained a host of features which were already archaic when the old maps were drawn.

In 1591 John Blagrave made a map of Feckenham in Worcestershire for the Queen and a copy of this map, which was made in 1744, survives. The village, lying about 5 miles (8 km) to the south-west of Redditch, had been a royal manor since AD 804 and was then surrounded by extensive tracts of hunting forest. As Clerk of Works to Richard II, Geoffrey Chaucer had rights in this forest in the 1380s. Not long after the commissioning of the map of the royal manor the area was disafforested, but the map shows the

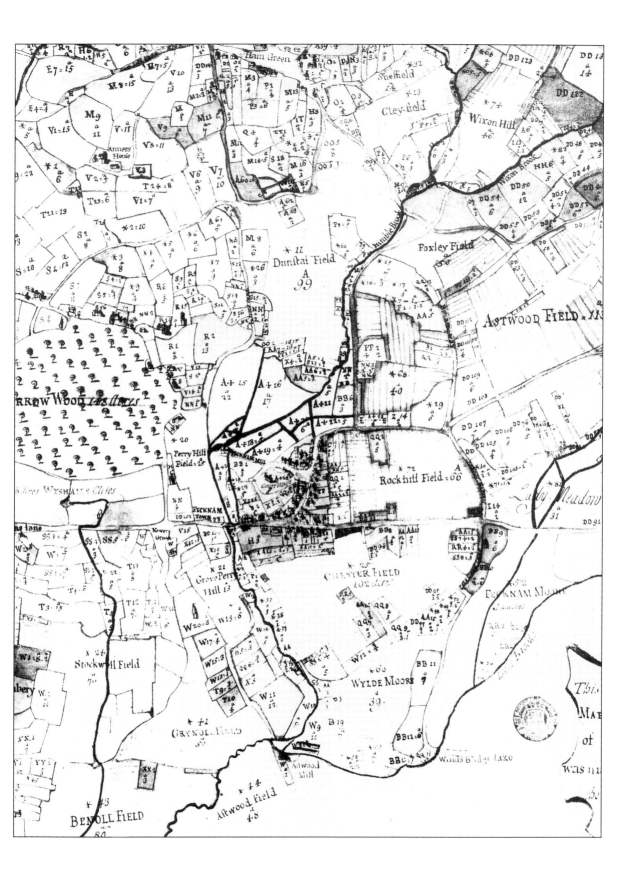

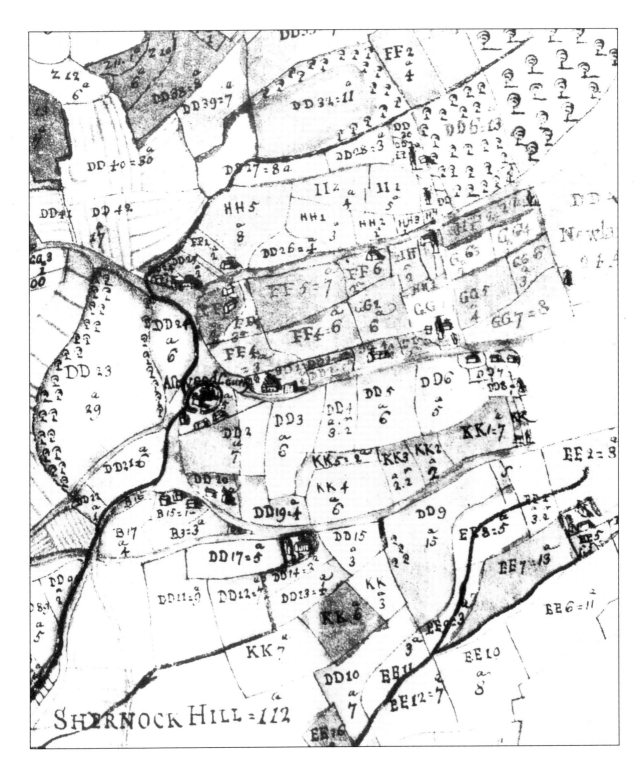

Court House buildings of the forest manor just to the west of the village square, traces of banked and moated enclosure being all that remains today.

The surrounding Elizabethan countryside is a wonderfully varied mosaic of coppices; wooded and open commons; open-field ploughland; field strips already enclosed by local agreements; little hedged pastures, many of them identified as assarts; common meadow; and parkland. Looking at this map of Feckenham as it existed four hundred years ago we discover a countryside devoid of any ugliness, a detailed tapestry of rural environments free of telegraph poles, conifers, pesticides, prairie fields, silage heaps, wind-blown fertiliser bags or any other modern afflictions.

The countryside displays characteristics of both ancient and champion types, but favours the former. Feckenham is a village with several open fields: Foxley Field, Astwood Field and Chester Field may have been the original open fields, but unenclosed plough strips are also shown in fields marked Shernock Hill, Rockhill Field and Dunstal Field, while other small strip fields occur further away from the village. This is certainly not an encounter with the 'three-field system' of the textbooks.

To complicate matters further, this estate is not dominated by a single village but shared between the village of Feckenham and various hamlets and scattered farmsteads. To the north of Feckenham trackways merge and broaden to form a green around which the dozen or so dwellings of the hamlet of Ham Green nestle, and Ham Green seems to have its own little clutch of strip fields, as does the loose, green-flanking village of Bradley Green to the west of Feckenham. In addition to the hamlets, several homesteads and farmsteads are scattered around the estate and stand serene within medieval moats. They probably represent superior farmsteads established during the recolonisation of the woodland. One of the most interesting, mapped four centuries ago and still surviving, is Astwood Court, a couple of miles to the north-east of Feckenham. The moated site dates from the fourteenth century and the original house was probably the royal hunting lodge of Feckenham Forest. Around the time that our map was drawn it was superseded by a farmhouse which became the seventeenth-century home of the celebrated herbalist, Nicholas Culpeper.

Not only do maps such as this provide us with very detailed pictures of the countryside at the time when they were drawn, they can also provide important clues to much older features. Just to the west of Feckenham is Berrow Wood and today the name survives in Berrowhill and Burial Lane. Such names, more commonly surviving as 'bury' or Borough, frequently denote Norman motte-and-bailey castles and there is good reason to suspect that Feckenham was indeed overlooked by such a castle. However, settlement here probably did not originate with the Norman castle or the

Opposite: detail from the Feckenham map showing the varied nature of the Elizabethan countryside around Astwood Court. The letters in the field denote the tenant farmers. Hereford and Worcester County Council.

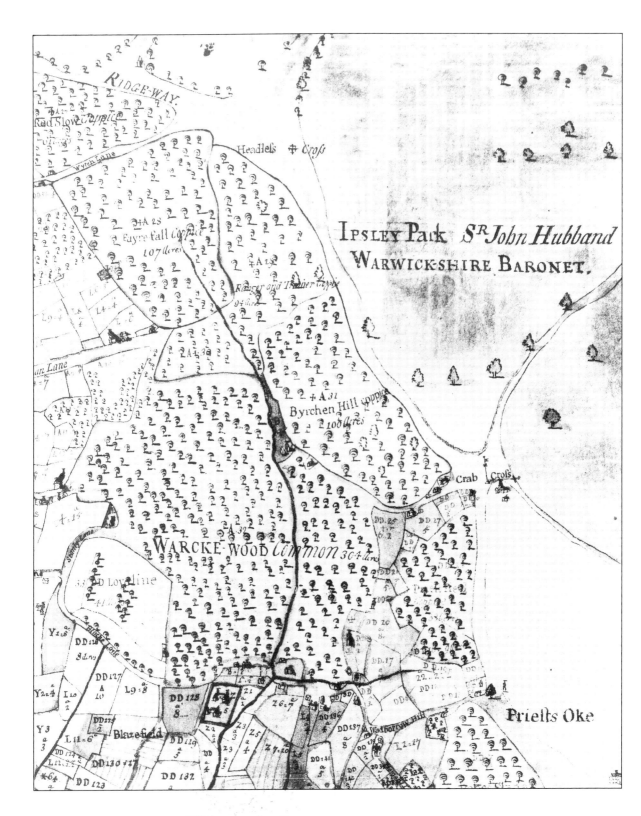

RIDGE-WAY.

Red Slow Coppice

Wytch Lane

Headless ✝ Cross

4 A 25
Fayre fall Coppice
107 Acres

4 A 26
Ranger and Trainer Coppice
94 Acres

IPSLEY PARK Sᴿ John Hubband
WARWICKSHIRE BARONET.

2 A 30

... Lane

2 · 4 A 31
Byrchen Hill Coppice
2 100 Acres

4 A 32

Crab Cross

DD 26

DD 27

Smith's Lane

WARCKE-WOOD Common 304 Acres

33 DD Love line

DD 29

DD 21

Black Lane

DD 20

Y 1 : 8

DD 114

DD 17

DD 15

Y 2 : 4   L 10

L 9 : 8

DD 128

Y 3

DD 112

L 11 : 6   Blazefield

DD 119

Watborow Hill

Prietts Oke

L 1 : 17

DD 130

DD 137

DD 123

DD 132

152

Saxon royal manor. The lane running east to west through the village is called Portway Lane on the map. It still serves the village but originated as a Roman road running from Droitwich to Stratford upon Avon (our cartographer could have followed its old course eastward for 10 miles (16 km) to visit Shakespeare in Stratford). Just to the south of Feckenham and its Roman Lane is the field named on the map as 'Chester Field'. Such names almost always derive from the Latin *castra*, a Roman army encampment or fort. So it is likely that the roots of Feckenham burrow down into the Roman period when a roadside fort, a small fortified town or a Romano-British settlement was established here.

Many of the old lanes and place-names around Feckenham still endure, but in some places the scene has been transformed. In the north of the map lanes and droves converge on an ancient ridgeway and an old headless cross is marked at the junction, the ridgeway being flanked by coppiced woodland to the west and the tree-studded lawns of Ipsley Park to the east. A couple of miles further south there is another junction of ridgeway and lanes and the cross and tiny hamlet of Crab Cross. Today the ridgeway exists as the busy A441 and Headless Cross and Crabbs Cross are populous suburbs of Redditch. Today, also, our only escape into *totally* unspoilt countryside is made with the imagination and an old map. In this way we can discover meadows spangled with wildflowers and woods ringing with birdsong. There are no rumbling juggernauts, no property developers, no screeching jets. The old map is a safer conveyance than a real time machine, for it does not put us in risk of the Black Death, religious persecution or any of the other hazards which were part and parcel of life in Shakespeare's England.

Numerous estate maps survive from the years around 1600 and they reveal how varied the Elizabethan countrysides were. In the Midland heartlands of open-field farming there were parishes which were largely blanketed in plough strips, where the whole arable empire focused on a single village, where piecemeal enclosure had made little progress and where outlying hamlets or farmsteads were few and far between. Strixton in Northamptonshire is an example. There were some places, like Gamlingay in Cambridgeshire, which did resemble the textbook models of peasant farming with open strip fields, common meadows and pastures and hedged closes. In areas like the Charnwood Forest, where much land had been wooded at the start of the Middle Ages, there were countrysides covered in a green patchwork of hedged assarts and there were also the ancient countrysides with their thickly hedged pastures that were often older than the Roman conquest, with their deep winding lanes, scattered farmsteads and hamlets and little strip fields which were slotted into the ancient framework.

The countryside shown on the Feckenham map illustrates a diversity that was also a feature of Elizabethan England at the regional scale. Mixed farming predominated; the pastoral farms needed some oats for fodder and barley for brewing and the arable farmers relied upon livestock to fertilise the fields where grain was grown. In the chalk downlands, sheep were pastured on the uplands by day and then folded on the fallowing ploughlands by night. Middlesex specialised on the cultivation of wheat for the London market, Cheshire on dairy produce – the county was already renowned for its cheese – and the northern uplands on producing coarse wool. Although each region had its commercial specialisations much still had to be produced for consumption in the cottage and farmhouse or on the manor. Villagers grew vegetables like carrots, cabbage, parsnips and turnips and most families kept a milk cow, while the lord had his dovecote and rabbit warren to supply fresh meat to his table.

Several Elizabethan writers lamented what they believed to be a crisis of woodland destruction. William Harrison (1534–93), the rector of Radwinter in Essex, wrote that 'Within these forty years we shall have little great timber growing'. In contrast, foreign visitors to south-eastern England who were accustomed to the bare expanses of farmland so often seen on the continent regarded the countryside as thickly wooded and hedged and a Frenchman remarked that 'in travelling you think you are in a continuous wood'. Most foreigners were impressed by the greenness of England, pasture, wood and hedgerow being more widespread than in their homelands. As in all other things the pattern varied from region to region. The real woodland crisis has occurred in the decades since the Second World War, when 50 per cent of our ancient lowland woodland has been destroyed. In Elizabethan times the demand for timber for the shipyards, iron foundries, glassworks and a host of other uses was great but the buoyant market generally ensured the careful management and re-planting of woodland. As coal was now becoming a significant fuel some of the pressure on the woods was lifted, with coal being exported by ship from Newcastle to London and the Low Countries. The poet, Michael Drayton (1563–1631), wrote:

> As of those mighty ships which in my mouth I bear,
> Fraught with my country coal of this Newcastle named,
> For which both far and near that place is no less famed
> Than India of her mines.

During the Elizabethan era, the wholesale destruction of villages and the conversion of their ploughlands into pasture (as described in the preceding chapter) gradually came to an end. Both government and popular opinion were determined that such ruthless evictions should stop, yet the 'privati-sation' of common land was still an active and controversial issue. Forces were at work which widened the gaps in the rural class system. William Harrison found that 'The ground of the parish is gotten up into a few men's hands, yea sometimes into the tenure of two or three, whereby the rest are compelled either to be hired servants unto the other or else to beg'. In fact he was witnessing the gradual drift from a feudal to a capitalist form of farming, with the changes coming much more swiftly to some parishes than to others. Most vulnerable to the forces of change were those with least land and least security of tenure. Cottagers depending on access to common grazing left the land when the lord enclosed or over-stocked the commons and small men were undermined when their more affluent neighbours agreed amongst each other to re-apportion and enclose the open plough strips.

Following the ravages of the Black Death the rural tenants and labourers who had survived benefited greatly from the shortage of men to work the land and the periodic onslaughts of disease kept population growth modest. In Elizabethan times, however, the population surged, growing by around 60 per cent between 1540 and 1610 to reach a level of over four million. Most towns grew even more rapidly, producing a rising demand for grain. In feudal days countless peasant families subsisted on holdings of around 15 acres (6.7 ha), producing just enough surplus to satisfy their obligations to lord and church. In the commercial climate of the Elizabethan age such holdings were no longer viable and even the tenants of much larger ones were often insecure. Agriculture was still by far the most important industry, but fewer and fewer families were gaining control of the countryside. Those squeezed out of their rural niches might seek work as farm labourers or join the march to the towns.

During Elizabeth's reign the population of London may have tripled. The tailor and historian, John Stow (c. 1525–1605), wrote in 1598 how the capital was rapidly expanding beyond its old walls: 'Hog Lane stretcheth north towards St Mary's Hospital without Bishopgate, and within these forty years had on both sides fair hedgerows of elm trees, with bridges and easy stiles to pass over into the pleasant fields [but is now] . . . made into a continual building throughout, of garden houses and small cottages . . .' Despite the vitality of town growth, by European standards Elizabethan England was a poorly urbanised realm. It has been estimated that of the thirty European cities with populations of more than 40,000, London was the only British example. The capital completely dwarfed all provincial centres, and in 1600, when London had around 200,000 inhabitants, Norwich, its nearest rival, had only about 15,000. Next came Bristol, York, Exeter, Newcastle and King's Lynn, while Birmingham, England's present

London as represented in an engraving by Cornelius Visscher which was completed shortly after the death of Elizabeth I. Only one bridge spanned the Thames and it was festooned with houses and wooden shops and stalls. Heads of 'traitors' have been put on spikes above the gateway, lower right. The Folger Shakespeare Library.

Billingsgate

Alhallows Barkin

Hackeny

Bridge Gate

157

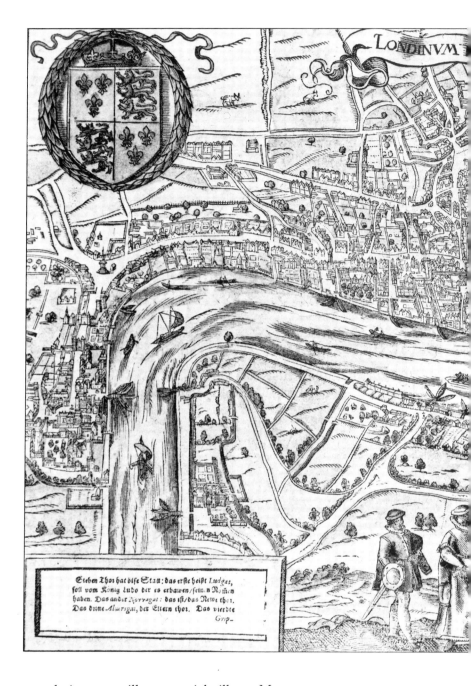

London around 1560 as portrayed in an engraving by Braun and Hogenberg. Mansell Collection.

second city, was still a manorial village. Most towns, even county towns, displayed many features of the overgrown village. Leicester, for example, was surrounded by its open fields, 2600 acres (*c.* 1050 ha) of ploughland, meadow and grazings in which many of the townspeople toiled in the manner of rustic peasants.

The great historian of the English landscape, Professor W. G. Hoskins,

158

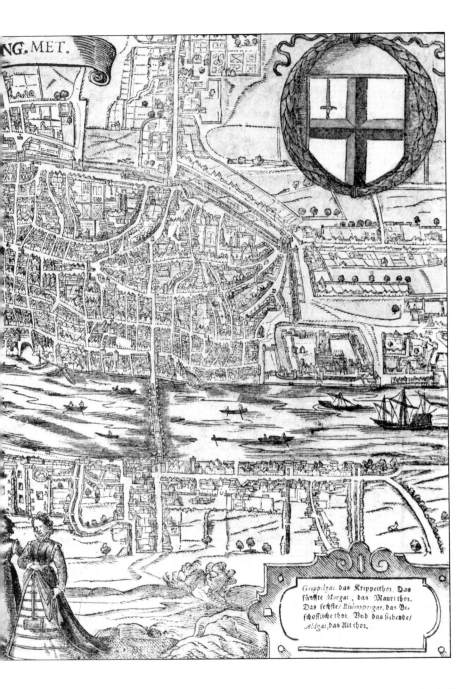

Grippelgat: das Krippeithor. Das
fünffte Morgat, das Maurithor.
Das sechste/ Bishoppeigat, das Bi-
schofflichethor. Vnd das sibende/
Aldgat, das Alt thor.

writes of the Elizabethan town that everything was on a miniature scale, 'all
except the quality of the people'. This was a time of great uncertainty, but
also a time of hope and expansion. Plague and famine still prowled the land
– the records show that twenty-five paupers starved to death in the streets
of Newcastle in the autumn of 1597. On the whole, however, population,
farm production and the economy all grew apace. These and other factors

nurtured a feeling of optimism in many hearts and this produced countless attempts at self-betterment. Such attempts are visible today in many surviving buildings of the Elizabethan period. The less grandiose examples are monuments to what Professor Hoskins called 'The Great Rebuilding'. Families of rural freeholders, copyholders and less impoverished tenants who participated in The Great Rebuilding often replaced a homestead that was crude, cramped and insubstantial with a new dwelling that was more spacious, workmanlike and built to endure. Farmhouses of some solidity were already occupied by the more substantial members of the Tudor rural community. One example, explored and reconstructed in its original form in a drawing by Peter F. Ryder, is the Netherfold farmhouse near Rotherham. It has been dated by a study of the tree rings of its original timbers to 1494–5. The dwelling measured 49 feet by 19 feet (15 by 6 m) and was divided into three bays. An open hall formed the central bay, while the flanking bays each had stairs leading up to upper chambers above, as shown in the cut-away drawing below. The building remained a farmhouse of some status until the end of the seventeenth century, when it was subdivided into cottages. Dwellings such as this which existed on the eve of the Great Rebuilding served in some ways as prototypes for those which followed. The movement began in the affluent south-east in the reign of

The Netherfold farmhouse as reconstructed by Peter F. Ryder.

Henry VIII (1509–47) and expanded so that it penetrated all the agricultural lowlands in the period about 1570–1640. It took longer to become established in the upland areas of livestock farming, where most of the surviving farmsteads concerned date from the late seventeenth and eighteenth centuries. In the lowland areas where grain farming was to the fore outbursts of rebuilding would follow seasons when high grain prices had brought a smile to the farmers' faces, while in lowland areas of livestock farming low bread grain prices seem to have allowed the country folk to make savings which could be invested in a new home.

The new dwellings were frequently framed in stout oak timbers with the panels of the timber frame filled in with wattle and daub. Sometimes they were of brick, widely used at Hull in the fourteenth century but still an expensive and prestigious material in most parts of Elizabethan England – though panels of brickwork often substituted for wattle and daub in the better houses. Although some places had local clay tile or pantile industries or quarried flagstones for roofing, thatching was almost universal. In some towns, like Bristol, it was banned to reduce the risk of fires – such as the one which gutted Norwich in the reign of Henry VII (and the ones which would consume most of London and Northampton in that of Charles II).

Two features gave the Elizabethan house both status and convenience: window glass and chimneys. An English glass-making industry had existed since the twelfth or thirteenth centuries and it was enormously stimulated by the arrival of skilled French, Flemish and Italian craftsmen around 1570. Fears that the industry was depleting woodland resources and had fallen into foreign hands did not prevent its growth, for the freedom to enjoy light without draught and chills was grasped by all who could afford to pay. Like most other innovations the building of chimneys diffused into the villages from the affluent districts of towns, and during Elizabeth's reign they increasingly became features of the rural domestic scene. They were often built to elaborate, eye-catching designs and on many of the estate maps of the time the cartographers can be seen to have gone to great pains to portray chimneys individually on the tiny dwellings that they drew. While many Elizabethan country folk were condemned to paupery by inflation, enclosure and profiteers there were others more fortunate who could now enjoy warmth and clean air though countless generations of their forebears had occupied dark, draughty, smoke-wreathed hovels.

Thousands of Elizabethan products of the Great Rebuilding survive. The dwellings were sturdy and in many lowland localities there were whole villages which were almost entirely rebuilt in the course of Elizabeth's reign. However, one may travel far and wide to discover an Elizabethan farmstead which has not been substantially modified during its long lifespan. Nowhere will one find an Elizabethan dwelling in an untouched

The Marriage Fête at Horsleydown by Joris Hoefnagel. By courtesy of The Marquis of Salisbury Courtauld Institute of Art.

163

164

Elizabethan setting. There are, however, some contemporary paintings which offer us more than passing glimpses and of which the most notable is Joris Hoefnagel's *The Marriage Fête at Horsleydown*. The guests with their brightly-coloured hose, trailing cloaks or long dresses seem oblivious to the mud beneath their feet and the near-morass extends right up to the walls of the nearby dwellings. Naturally there are no asphalt highways, telephone wires, parked vehicles and so on to intrude upon the vista and in consequence the houses seem to nestle into the scene as few nestle today. Looking more closely at the scene painted by this Flemish traveller we see roofs of thatch or of russet clay tiles and walls of oak and wattle and daub or of brick; lovers and archers sport in the pastures, a team of horses haul a cart along a rutted lane and the prisoner in the stocks is sheltered by a flimsy projection of thatch. The scene is set not in some idyllic English backwater but in the vicinity of Bermondsey. In the distance we see the busy Thames and beyond it the Tower of London – reminders that even in the most vital and urbanised part of the realm the countryside was close at hand. Today London and its suburbs extend fifteen miles southwards beyond this rustic scene.

The countryside of Elizabethan times contained much to gladden the eye of a modern conservationist. In this sixteenth-century illustration of September by Simon Benninck we see a newly-laid hedgerow in the middle distance which is punctuated by 'maidens' which will be allowed to grow tall as timber trees. Harrowing and ploughing take place in the foreground and to the left pigs enjoy the 'pannage' of an oak wood. The swineherds are dislodging acorns with sticks. Victoria & Albert Museum.

CHAPTER THIRTEEN

Rob Roy's Scotland

ROB ROY MACGREGOR BELONGED TO one of the Scottish Highlands' most feared and unruly clans: the Macgregor territory being on the borders of Argyll. Under James VI of Scotland, who became James I of England, the clan name was outlawed; it was re-instated after the Reformation in recognition of the Macgregors' loyalty to the Stuart kings, though in 1695 the clan name was again proscribed. At the start of the eighteenth century Rob Roy was a cattle dealer, but following a disputed debt to the Duke of Montrose he found himself an outlaw. He established his base on the Braes of Balquidder and was resolved to cause Montrose as much discomfort as possible. This he achieved to the extent that he is remembered as the Scottish equivalent of Robin Hood; whether or not he really did redistribute the Duke's wealth among his poor tenants as frequently as the legends suggest he was certainly a real historical figure – and unlike most outlaws he is believed to have died in his bed at the age of almost eighty.

The Scotland that Rob Roy knew was little like the Scotland of today. Within years of his passing it had embarked on a rapid and painful transformation so that Rob Roy was the last player in a long tradition of banditry and insurgency. He was the last outlaw and one of the last witnesses to the old Highland ways. Were he able to return to the scenes of his exploits he would surely regard them as desolate wastelands and gaze in disbelief at the empty places which were once the abodes of his neighbours and countrymen.

The pacification of the Scottish landscape had proceeded more slowly and sporadically than elsewhere in Britain. Much of the Mesolithic activity was confined to shorelines, where small migratory bands moved from one strand to the next, fishing and gathering molluscs, whose discarded shells gradually accumulated in great mounds or 'middens'. In the Neolithic period agricultural communities became established in the more fertile farming environments in the coastal plains and valleys, perhaps beginning as pastoral farmers and gradually adopting cereal cultivation. Even on the cold and windblasted slopes of Shetland stones were gathered from the land and piled in cairns or incorporated in walls around the grain fields. In

Opposite: a romanticised Victorian representation of Rob Roy shown in the Highland dress which had been developed during the Queen's sentimental infatuation with Scotland. In reality the outlaw would have worn no such elaborate sporran, his kilt would have been much shorter and would have been an integral part of the heavy woollen plaid which served as a cloak and blanket. Scottish tartans were also systematised in Victoria's reign. BBC Hulton Picture Library.

ROB ROY'S SCHOTTISCHE,

some places the forest clearance and settlement was destined to be permanent, while in others the soils became exhausted and the woodland returned. During the Bronze Age the pace of colonisation appears to have quickened, although in many places the old shifting tradition of cultivation was still practised, with land being cleared, cultivated and then abandoned. Countrysides patterned by networks of small fields appeared in some parts of southern Scotland, while during the Iron Age many more such countrysides were created.

In the Highlands, however, the great Caledonian Forest remained largely intact, with only the higher peaks and watersheds emerging through the blanket of Scots pine. After around AD 400 the conversion to farmland of wildwood and regenerated woodland became widespread and permanent in Scotland, but even these colonisations seem only to have nibbled the edges of the forest in the Highlands.

During the Middle Ages royal hunting forests comparable to those existing in Robin Hood's England were established. These forests of pine and birch were, however, much wilder than the mosaics of deciduous woodland and farmland of which most English forests were composed. Two Scottish Kings, James II and James III, were kidnapped whilst hunting in the fastnesses of their forests. In the south of Scotland monastic flocks were introduced and many formerly wooded areas were converted into sheep pastures. In the Highlands, however, the country consisted of expanses of natural pine and birch forest; places where the forest was deliberately destroyed to remove the refuges of robber bands, and other areas where woodland was in short supply.

The economy of the Highlands was based on the production, sale and theft of black cattle. These cattle were driven southwards to markets in the lowlands of Scotland, resold and then driven to English markets via drove roads which traversed the Pennine spine of northern England. The trade was established in medieval times but was periodically disrupted by Anglo-Scottish wars, whilst rustlers posed a continuous threat to the herds as they advanced southwards through the glens and passes of the Highlands. After the Act of Union of 1707 had put Anglo-Scottish relations on a firmer footing the cattle trade blossomed and the market or 'tryst' centres of Crieff and Falkirk rose in importance. In 1723 some 30,000 cattle are said to have been sold to English drovers at Crieff. As a cattle dealer, Rob Roy would have known this trade well.

Deer hunting rose to a crescendo of organised slaughter at the start of the seventeenth century. The English travel writer, John Taylor, described a 'Tinchel' or hunt which he attended in the Braemar area which lasted for twelve days and involved up to 1500 beaters. He saw eighty red deer slain in the space of two hours but claimed to have seen neither a house nor an

inhabitant after passing Kindrochet castle at the start of the hunt. After the death of James VI in 1625, however, the royal forests were largely sold to private owners. It was about this time that commercial forestry began in the Scottish Highlands. In 1830 Sir T. D. Lander described seeing some gigantic decaying trees in Invernessshire and he may have been one of the last people to set eyes on a remnant of untouched British wildwood. Some woods were cleared to extend the cattle grazings or destroyed by the clansmen's goats while others were felled; in Abernethy forest in 1728 some 60,000 pine were felled to provide masts for the navy and when they were judged too small for the role they were burned for charcoal. Iron works were established at a number of locations in the forests, the ore being imported and trees removed for miles around to provide the fuel for smelting.

Most parts of the Highlands did not resemble the wilderness described by John Taylor, for the land was far more heavily populated than today. The clansmen were peasant farmers occupying scattered hamlets or *clachans* and the better land in the vicinity of the *clachan* was divided into plough strips, heavily manured and continuously cropped. Beyond this 'in-field' land was 'out-field' land, parts of which were periodically cropped to exhaustion and then grazed as pasture for several years until their fertility had recovered. All around the cultivated area lay expanses of poorer grazing and woodland, with many members of each community

A cattle drover of Rob Roy's time on the flanks of the Ochils bound for the Falkirk tryst. BBC Hulton Picture Library.

169

leaving the *clachan* each year at the onset of summer to occupy temporary huts or 'shielings' situated amongst the upland or island grazings.

The peasants were clansmen and women who owed total allegiance to their chieftain. The origins of the Scottish clan system are lost in the mists of time, but the members of the clan were united by belief in descent from a common forefather. The Macgregor clan, for example, claimed descent from Grogar, son of King Kenneth McAlpin who was crowned in AD 843 after his Scottish subjects had overwhelmed the ancient Pictish kingdom. The origins of the clan founders were diverse, the Frasers and Gordons having Norman ancestry and so it is plain that some clans were still forming during the Middle Ages. The Macleods had Viking origins while the Mackintoshes and Macphersons claimed Pictish ancestors.

Within each territory the clan chieftain ruled as a virtual monarch. Each clan had its own rules and customs and the power of the chief over his subjects was absolute. The clansmen were both peasants and warriors who could be mustered at any notice to follow the chief to war. Land was held by the chief, sublet to petty nobles or 'tacksmen' and then sublet and sublet again on short leases to peasant tenants. Since wealth was held in cattle and status measured according to the number of armed clansmen that a chieftain could muster the Highlands became both over-grazed and over-populated.

Rob Roy's Scotland was a museum of tribal life. To the south of the great fault line which marks the boundary of the Highlands the land was pacified and peopled by settled farmers who spoke a lowland Scots dialect of English. To the north lay a land of feuds and famines, the domain of real monarchs of the glen whose loyalty to the crowns of Scotland or England was seldom more than nominal but who presided over vast armies of Gaelic-speaking subjects.

The defeat of the Jacobite clans at Culloden in 1746 marked the end of Rob Roy's Scotland. The clansmen were disarmed and then evicted, for in the decades following Culloden vast flocks of sheep were introduced on the old forest land, cattle grazings and in-fields and the Highlands became a desert. Today little more than two centuries after the evictions or 'clearances' began, the Scotland of Rob Roy is as dead as the England of Robin Hood.

The Georgian Era: The Privatisation of the Countryside

DURING THE GEORGIAN PERIOD (1714–1830) the English countrysides grew to maturity. Most of them preserved features inherited from many earlier periods, but in scores of places which have escaped the worst ravages of recent times the rural scenes which we enjoy today are quite largely the creations of the Georgian age. This age witnessed the first stirrings of the Industrial Revolution, generally held to have begun around 1760, the rapid growth of towns and the transformation of countless countrysides.

Previously, changes in the rural parishes had been gradual and were accomplished by the yeomen and peasants who toiled upon the land. The great lords and lesser gentry did not usually become deeply involved in the details of farming and were generally mainly interested in the harvesting of rents and services rather than of crops. Very gradually, however, attitudes changed. As early as 1600 Thomas Wilson observed that 'The gentlemen, which were wont to addict themselves to the wars, are now for the most part grown to become good husbands [farmers], and know well how to improve their lands to the utmost as the farmer or countryman, so that they take their farms into their hands as the leases expire . . .' The changes in Georgian England were unusual in that now change was usually imposed on the landscape by the greater landowners themselves rather than resulting from the day-to-day labours of their humble tenants and hirelings. For the first time men of wealth and position chose to express their status, power and affluence by reshaping the fabric of the countryside.

This was made possible by the concentration of the ownership of land in greater and greater estates. During the Elizabethan period, as we have seen, the lords of manors and the greater yeomen had tended to increase their holdings at the expense of the lesser lights in the village society. Now, however, the tendency was for land to become concentrated in great estates. Such estates were held by men who were sufficiently wealthy to be able to experiment with the latest innovations in farming, to survive the disruptions wrought by change and to withstand short-term losses in order to enjoy the long-term gains. Rich men could weather a crisis of poor farm profits and buy cheap land when their poorer neighbours went under, while when farming was booming they were the ones who benefited most. Although their pockets were deep such men often spent heavily in order to maintain their status, so estates which were well organised and profitable were needed to underwrite the extravagant lifestyles.

The men who manipulated the landscape came from a variety of backgrounds. Some were members of the old landed aristocracy, some members of the nobility who had profited greatly from official appointments at court and in government, and some had acquired and expanded estates following the great sell-off of monastic land after the Dissolution of the Monasteries, while others still were descended from prudent and ambitious yeomen who had for generations engaged in enlarging their lands. Then, as industrialisation gathered pace, established landowners who owned mines and quarries could plough their profits into the acquisition of more land. Meanwhile, newly rich industrialists could wed their wealth to status and finance the revitalisation of a decrepit estate or become powers in the countryside by buying up adjacent farms until a new rural empire had come into being. Near the capital members of the old

The days of the crowded fields. Detail from a painting by an unknown artist around 1700 of a countryside near Cheltenham. The fields are full of harvest workers while morris dancers perform in the foreground. Note too the richly hedged pastures in the distance. The mechanisation of farming which gained impetus in Victorian times gradually emptied the crowded fields. Cheltenham Art Gallery and Museums.

class of landed gentry were being displaced as landowners by affluent businessmen; Daniel Defoe remarked on the changes as early as 1724.

Gradually a distinctive Georgian landscape materialised in district after district. At its heart there was the mansion, more likely than not a vast status-proclaiming symbol built or rebuilt in one of the fashionable classical styles. Around the mansion were the sprawling acres of manicured parkland, while beyond the walled confines of the park lay estate lands with geometrical patterns of young hedgerows defining fields in which the latest notions about crops and crop rotations were being put to the test.

Edward II (1307–27) had been ridiculed for his interest in the rural crafts of hedging and thatching, but George III (1760–1820) was 'Farmer George'; he contributed articles to the *Annals of Agriculture* and inaugurated a model farm at Windsor. He was not immune from ridicule but his enthusiasm for farming was a factor which endeared him to his subjects. The Agricultural Revolution began before the Industrial Revolution – it paved the way for industrialisation by helping to provide the surplus of produce needed to support a growing population of craftsmen, artisans and factory workers. The revolution on the land did not always involve the adoption of new discoveries, but rather it flourished under an attitude of mind – or an attitude of the upper-class mind – which encouraged the expansion and improvement of existing farming practices.

Clover was grown as cattle fodder in the seventeenth century but its beneficial effects on the soil were not appreciated. Then the 2nd Viscount Townshend, who developed an interest in farming on his estate at Raynham in Norfolk after 1730, included it in his acclaimed four-course crop rotation of turnips, barley or oats, clover and wheat. 'Turnip Townshend' did not invent the crop rotation; turnips, rye grass and legumes like clover, trefoil and sainfoin were rotated on the Duke of Grafton's Northamptonshire estates in the 1720s while the old open-field farming system was organised so as to allow one great field to fallow each year. Medieval farmers also realised that the importation of new blood would improve their livestock even though they did not understand the concept of hybrid vigour. Robert Bakewell of Dishley in Leicestershire took a rather different approach to stock breeding by seeking to develop uniform breeds. Then, as breeds standardised so landowners could compete to produce the finest specimen of each breed. While the Tudor or Elizabethan magnate might decorate his rooms with tapestries depicting the beast of the chase, his Georgian descendant was likely to display portraits of himself posing beside his prize shorthorn bull or new Leicester ram.

One change begat another, with the incorporation of clover and root crops in rotations providing winter feed for livestock and allowing better

The agricultural innovator Coke of Holkham posing with his improved sheep. BBC Hulton Picture Library.

but more demanding new strains of animal to be supported. In 1776 squire Coke of Holkham in Norfolk inherited a run-down estate but drained and manured the poor light soil and succeeded in cultivating wheat. He also studied the nutritional aspects of different types of grass and experimented with the selective breeding of sheep and cattle. So well was his work attuned to the spirit of the age that as many as 7000 farmers would assemble to attend his agricultural gatherings.

The enthusiasm for progress and experimentation did not always permeate the lower classes of rural society. A family which would hope to subsist from one year to the next by adhering to the traditional and proven farming practices could not be expected to jeopardise their survival by adopting some new-fangled notion. Moreover, open-field farming of an essentially medieval type still held sway over much of lowland England. The small copyholder and tenant frequently had his activities closely intermeshed in the complexities of communal farming practices and was not free to experiment even if he wished to do so.

It was inevitable that the confrontation between progress and power on

174

the one hand and tradition on the other would have traumatic consequences. We have already seen how the old system of open-field farming was gradually being dismantled in many parishes as leading groups of tenants and freeholders cobbled together local agreements about the amalgamation of strips and the enclosure of common land. Now, however, the greater landowners and the advocates of progress were seeking the wholesale destruction of a method of farming which had, for all its faults, endured for a thousand years. Parliamentary Enclosure became the instrument which would transform the landscape and communal life in a multitude of parishes. Leading landowners owning four-fifths or more of the land in a parish would petition Parliament to produce an Act of Enclosure and then commissioners were appointed to oversee the allocation of land. The commissioners, their surveyors and valuer sought to unravel the surviving pattern of plough strips and commons and create a new .division which would furnish every lawful claimant with a new consolidated holding which was equivalent to the fragmented lands and rights to the common which existed before enclosure.

The first Act enclosed the parish of Radipole in Dorset in 1604 but was not recognised as a landmark in the history of the countryside. The final Act occurred in 1914, by which time around 5400 Acts had affected about

Averham Park in Nottinghamshire as painted by an unknown artist around 1720. The hilltop mansion standing in parkland dominates the scene while in the foreground we see ridge and furrow ploughland looking much as it had in medieval times. Good representations of ridge and furrow are seldom found in illustrations. John Harris.

Geometrical wall pattern of the Parliamentary enclosure era in Nidderdale. Richard Muir.

7 million acres (2,832,861 ha) of common land. The movement was most active in the period 1750–1850, particularly during the wars with France when domestic grain prices rose because of difficulties in importing corn, some 3200 Acts being passed during the reign of George III.

Parliamentary enclosure was probably the most influential single event in the moulding of the countryside. In the parishes affected it added a new geometrical dimension to the landscape. The fields produced were the creations of surveyors rather than of gradual agricultural evolution. The conditions of the awards demanded the hedging or walling of the prescribed fieldscape, usually according to detailed specifications. In the lowlands some 200,000 miles (321,870 km) of new hedgerow were planted while in the uplands arrow-straight walls partitioned the old commons. Today, wherever one sees rectangular fields bounded by straight walls or hedgerows it is much more likely than not that the countryside is a Georgian legacy. The changes affected the use as well as the partitioning of land. Frequently the old ploughlands became pastures, while within his new compact little realm the farmer could adopt the fashionable crop rotations rather than being meshed into the communal practice. Meanwhile in the uplands, land enclosed from the common moor was often ploughed a few times, limed and converted into pasture, with stones

176

turned-up during ploughing being assimilated into the new field walls.

In Georgian times, and again today, progress was often interpreted as being what was good for the prosperous classes rather than for the national community as a whole. There is no doubt that it caused great hardship and suffering and it tolled the death knell for the old peasant class. The agricultural commentator, Arthur Young, advocated enclosure and realised that the traditional ways of holding land placed great obstacles in the path of progress. Nonetheless he could not deny that 'by nineteen out of twenty Enclosure Acts the poor are injured, and most grossly'. After enclosure there was likely to be an exodus from the village. Gone would be the commoners and cottagers who scraped a living from the common but received nothing in the award because they lacked any rights in the meadow and ploughland. Soon gone would be the recipients of tiny holdings who had lost access to the common, could not afford the cost of hedging and fencing and could not subsist on the legacy of what was, in effect, a privatisation of communal resources. Other villagers made a happier retreat from the village, leaving an old village farmstead for a newly built one established within the new and compact endowment of rectangular fields. Sometimes the old farmstead was partitioned into cottages to accommodate farm workers, some of these workers being peasant farmers

Simon Manby's reconstruction drawing of Roystone Grange in Derbyshire shortly after the early nineteenth-century enclosure award. Gangs of drystone wallers are at work in the fields transferring the award from the map to the landscape.

Holkham Hall in Norfolk, a Palladian mansion standing within a landscaped park epitomises the spirit of the eighteenth century. It was built in the 1730s and was the home of the great agricultural reformer, Coke of Holkham, the first Earl of Leicester. Richard Muir.

broken by enclosure and now obliged to sell their labour. In such ways our familiar countrysides of straight-edged fields and scattered Georgian and Victorian farmsteads came into being.

The power centres of the Georgian realm were the great country houses. The Georgians did not invent the stately mansion; the medieval kings had their palaces and during the Tudor era aristocrats began to migrate from draughty castles to great houses as strong government imposed peace upon the kingdom. It was in the Georgian age, however, that houses built to an unprecedented degree of magnificence proliferated. These buildings reflected profound changes in attitudes to society. The medieval hall was the government offices, social centre, restaurant, court room and capital of a community all rolled into one. There the lord received his subordinates, dispensed justice, entertained his inferiors to lavish feasts and discussed the financial affairs of the estate. But as the years rolled by the bonds between the lord and his inferiors weakened. The landlords became more interested in establishing some influence at the royal court, in obtaining privacy at home and in exploiting and developing their houses in ways which would impress their social equals rather than the lesser lights of the locality. They perceived themselves as members of the ruling establishment and attempted to cultivate an interest in classical scholarship. The product of all this was the eruption of scores of mansions, each one lavishly endowed with both public and private suites of rooms with segregated accommodation for the servants, and the great majority of them were built according to Greek or Roman architectural principles. Some of these outlooks were incorporated in the farmsteads of the more affluent farmers. The farmhouses which mushroomed after enclosure often had fashionably symmetrical facades and the farm servants were no longer accommodated in the upper storey of the house, but banished to separate cottages.

In his hall the medieval lord sought little privacy and was in close contact with subordinates of all kinds; tenants, servants, retainers and poorer relations. The growing gulf of isolation between the classes came to be expressed in the countryside. More likely than not the Georgian mansion was set in a vast park of silent and artificial countryside which was carefully manicured according to contemporary tastes. The landscaped park not only announced to distinguished guests that their host was a man of gentility, it also served as a *cordon sanitaire*, insulating the landed gentry from the tenants who created the wealth which allowed them to maintain their extravagant lifestyles.

Wentwood Woodhouse in South Yorkshire, an illustration from a Humphry Repton Red Book showing how the park would appear when his landscaping work was complete. Sheffield City Libraries.

Expanses of empty and unworked countryside seldom existed and so many park-making projects began with the eviction of those who lived within the designated confines. Sometimes the unfortunates were cast out upon the road and sometimes they were removed to custom-built estate villages. If such villages were established just outside the park gates or on an approach road and likely to be seen by people of quality they might well consist of cottages which had been titivated with the provision of porches, fancy barge boards or the arms or monogram of the landlord. Villagers at Shugborough in Staffordshire and Wimpole in Cambridgeshire were obliged to move more than once as the great park was progressively expanded. When the village was moved its medieval church was often left stranded in the park, where it frequently became increasingly so overrun by monuments to the noble family living near by that the visitor might wonder whether it existed to glorify God or the landowning dynasty.

During the Georgian and early Victorian periods the English country-side came of age. In the nineteenth century classical architecture yielded to fantastic, rambling parodies of the Gothic style as the mighty, having reinforced the social segregation of society, looked back whimsically to the social coherence of a mythical medieval golden age. In the countryside the main contrast between Georgian and late Victorian times concerned the numbers of people seen toiling on the land. In the early eighteenth century horsedrawn seed drills and hoes were developed by Jethro Tull, but the wholesale mechanisation of farming was a feature of the Victorian Age. As machines replaced hands and hand tools so the fields and the villages became emptier.

Many of those who had lost their footholds in the countryside because of enclosure or mechanisation resorted to the towns, many of which were expanding rapidly under the stimulus of industrialisation. At the start of the nineteenth century a five-minute stroll from Liverpool Town Hall would take one into cornfields – yet by 1851 the pressure of growth and immigration were so great that thousands of people there were living in cellars and the Health Committee had some 10,000 of these cellars cleared and filled up with sand. Georgian England was a realm of country towns and county towns. Norwich, with a population of around 30,000, was the only town apart from London of real size, but by the end of Victoria's reign Britain contained more than 80 towns with more than 50,000 inhabitants.

The Georgian period witnessed a revolution in transport as well as in agriculture and industry. The development of the railway network mainly came later, but for the first time the kingdom acquired a road network which was superior to the one existing in Roman times. In 1663 an Act was passed which allowed the Justices in three Midlands counties to finance repairs to the Great North Road by the levying of tolls on road users. Like

the first Act of Parliamentary Enclosure this was not recognised at the time as a great historical landmark, but by the close of the Georgian era more than 20,000 miles (32,000 km) of highway had been built or improved by the different local turnpike trusts and workmanlike roads punctuated by little roadside toll houses had become part of the English scene. By this time the railways were beginning to serve notice that the coaching age would be overtaken by the age of the train. Nonetheless, the creation of turnpikes and of an efficient system of stage coaches had done much to bind the realm by shrinking internal distances. In 1754 it took four and a half days to travel from London to Manchester and by 1825 the journey could be accomplished in less than 24 hours. Meanwhile a canal system was developing to assemble industrial materials at factory sites and to disperse the manufactured products.

It would be wonderful to be able to conclude by saying that the modern

The High Street in Lincoln as depicted in a lithograph by I. Haghe around 1835 is a mixture of elegance and rusticity. The cathedral rises in the distance and the stylish building in the right foreground is a conduit, providing the citizens with drinking water. From the Local Studies Collection, Lincoln Library, by courtesy of Lincolnshire Library Service.

age is adding the finishing touches to countrysides which have been evolving for thousands of years. Sadly, rather than gilding the rural lily we are obliterating landscapes which were thousands of years in the making. Since 1947 we have lost 95 per cent of wildflower meadows; 60 per cent of lowland heaths; 80 per cent of downland sheep walks; 50 per cent of ancient woodlands and some 200,000 miles (*c.* 320,000 km) of hedgerow. Ironically all this destruction has taken place at a time when popular enthusiasm for the countryside is at its highest level ever. But if those in power really meant what they mouth about conservation would Sites of Special Scientific Interest really be facing destruction at a rate of 10 per cent every year? In this book carefully executed reconstruction drawings have been used to evoke the appearance of former countrysides. If the current rates of devastation continue for just a few more decades then reconstruction drawings will be needed to tell us what unspoiled countryside looked like.

Index

Agricultural Revolution 173
Alcuin 96
Alfred, King 86, 95, 97–8
Anglo Saxon Chronicle 97, 103–4, 115
Anglo-Saxon 'invasion' 74–5, 77–8
animals, wild 7–14, 30, 53, 118, 121
  domestication 15, 19
Arden, Forest of 125–7
Arthur, King 75–6
assarting 125–7, 146, 153
Astwood Court (Worcs) 151
Augustine, Saint 88, 90
Avebury (Wilts) 24–7, 30–2

Bakewell, Robert 173
Ballynagilly (Co. Tyrone) 20
Barton Court Farm (Oxon) 77
Bede, Venerable 142
birds 9
Birmingham 155, 158
Black Death (Great Plague) 135, 139–43, 145–6
Bloodaxe, Erik 101
bracken 27, 29–30
Bristol 155, 161
burhs 97–8
burial practices
  Bronze Age 40–2
  Dark Ages 82–3
  Iron Age 55–6
  Neolithic period 27–8, 32–3
Burton Agnes (Yorks) 117
Butser Ancient Farm Project 52

Caesar, Julius 57–8, 76
cairns 35–6
Canterbury 62

Carn Brea (Cornwall) 21–5
Chalton (Hants) 80–1
Chaucer, Geoffrey: *The Canterbury Tales* 135–9, 147, 148
Chichester 98
Chilgrove (Sussex) 68–71
chimneys in Tudor times 161
Chisbury Camp (Wilts) 98
churches 89–95
Cistercian monks 129–30
civitas 62
clans, Scottish 166, 169–70
Clay Lane (Northants) 52, 66–7
Coke, Thomas, 1st Earl of Leicester 174
Colchester 61–2
Colloquy of Abbot Aelfric of Eynsham (*c.* AD1000) 102
coloniae 57, 61–2
common land 87, 90, 108–9, 127, 146–7, 155, 176–7
  see also enclosures
copper working 40
Cowdery's Down (Hants) 82–3
Credenhill Camp (Welsh Marches) 46
Cricklade (Wilts) 98
Croft Ambrey hillfort (Hereford/Worcs) 44–6
Cro Magnons 11–12
crops 23–4, 27, 30, 54, 77, 83, 111, 154, 174
  rotation 173

Danebury (Hants) 46
Danelaw 95

Dartmoor 34–40
Darwin, Charles 13
Davenport, Sir John de 123
deer parks 123–4
Defoe, Daniel 173
Domesday Book (AD1086) 103–18
Drayton, Michael 4, 154
Drizzlecombe (Dartmoor) 36
Dunston's Clump (Notts) 78–80
dwellings
  Bronze Age 36–40
  Dark Age 78–85
  Elizabethan era 160–5
  Iron Age 43–54
  Middle Ages 114, 116–18, 133, 138–9
  in middle and late Saxon period 98–100
  in Roman Britain 59, 66–71, 77

Earls Barton church tower (Northants) 92
Edward I 134
Edward II 173
Edwy, King 89
enclosure(s)
  Bronze Age 36
  in Georgian period 175–8
  in Middle Ages 127, 146–7
  in Roman Britain 60–1
  in Tudor times 155
evictions of peasants in Tudor times 145–7, 154–5
Exeter 62, 98, 155

farming, establishment of 20, 24, 27

farmsteads
  Bronze Age 39–40
  in Dark Ages 78–80, 84
  in Georgian period 177–9
  Iron Age 43, 50–4
  in Middle Ages 131
  in Roman Britain 60–1, 67
  in Tudor times 151, 160
Feckenham (Worcs) 148–54
Fens, reclamation of 127–9
fish(ing) 15, 19, 83, 101
food 15–16, 18–19, 24, 78–9, 100–1, 154
Forest Charter (AD1217) 124, 125
Forest Law 120–7
forests 20–1, 101, 120–8, 168–9
fortifications
  Bronze Age 39–40
  Iron Age 43–50
  in Saxon times 97–8
  in Roman Britain 66, 68, 73

Gamlingay (Cambs) 153
George III ('Farmer George') 173
Gildas 76
glass-making 161
Gloucester 61
Goltho (Lincs) 116
Gomeldon (Wilts) 116
grange system of dispersed farms 130
Grauballe Man 56
Grimspound (Dartmoor) 37–8

hamlets 50, 78–80, 84, 145
Hampsthwaite (Yorks) 134
Harrison, William 154–5

183

Harrying of the North (AD1069–71) 114–16, 129
hedgerows 39, 87–8, 113, 173, 176
destruction of 182
Helman Tor (Cornwall) 23
Henry II 124
Henry III 124, 125
Hesterton (Yorks) 81–3, 85
hillforts 43–50
Holme Moor (Dartmoor) 37–8
Holt, Professor J.C. 119
Hood, Robin (Robert Hod) 119–20
Hoskins, Professor W.G. 131, 158–60
Hull 161
hunting 15, 18–19, 24, 30, 83, 168–9

Industrial Revolution 171–3, 180
infant mortality 28, 82–3, 101
Ipswich 97, 132

John, King 124, 132

King's Lynn 155

Langland, William: The Vision of Piers Plowman (c. AD1377) 119, 135–6, 138–9, 146–7
Langport (Somerset) 98
Laws of King Ine of Wessex (c. AD690) 86–7
lead mining 58, 60, 110
Leicester 158
life expectancy 28, 78, 83, 101
Lincoln 61–5, 85, 110, 181
Lindow Man 55–6
Littlecote Park (Wilts) 71
Llantwit Major (South Glamorgan) 67–8
London 61, 78, 110, 132, 155–9
Long Ash Hill (Dartmoor) 36

Macgregor, Rob Roy 166–8

Maiden Castle (Dorset) 46–50
manors
in Middle Ages 131–2
Norman 105, 116–17
mansions, Georgian 173, 178–80
see also dwellings
maps, medieval 148, 151, 153
markets, medieval 132, 134
Merrivale (Dartmoor) 36
Mesolithic period 14–19, 34, 166
Midsummer Hill (Welsh Marches) 46
moats 131
Moel-y-Gaer (Glwyd) 50
monasteries 129–30, 134, 168, 172
More, Sir Thomas: Utopia 146
Morris, Richard 133
Mucking (Essex) 40
municipii 61–2

Neanderthal Man 6, 8, 10–11
Neolithic period 20–33, 34, 166–7
Netherfold farm (Yorks) 160
Neville, Alan de 120
Newcastle 155
Norwich 110, 132, 155, 161, 180

open-field farming 90, 109–13, 125, 146, 153, 173–5
Overton Hill (Wilts) 31

Paviland Cave (Gower) 11–12
'Pete Marsh' (Lindow Man) 55–6
Pickering Vale (Yorks) 14
Pimperne House (Dorset) 51–2
plagues 135, 139–42, 145, 159
Plym Valley (Dartmoor) 34–6, 38
population 58, 76, 78, 84,

86, 105, 125–7, 133, 139, 143, 145, 155, 169, 173
see also Black Death
pottery 23, 28, 32

Rackham, Oliver 87–8, 106–10
Raunds church (Northants) 94–5
reaves 36
reclamation of wetlands 128–9
'Red Lady' 11–12
religious beliefs/practices
Bronze Age 40–1
Dark Ages 82
Iron Age 46, 55
in middle and late Saxon period 88–90, 95, 101
in Neanderthal times 11–12
in Neolithic period 24, 28–9
in Roman Britain 71–2
Rivenhall Church (Essex) 93–4
road systems 61–2, 68, 73, 85, 137–8, 153, 180–1
Rob Roy (Macgregor) 166–8
Rodwell, W. and K. 93
Roman occupation 43, 46, 49, 54, 57–73
Rous, John 145–6
Roystone Grange (Derbyshire) 58–61, 130–1, 177

St Albans (Verulamium) 62
Saxons 77–82, 84–5, 88
Scotland in the eighteenth century 166–70
Shaugh Moor (Dartmoor) 34–5
Silbury Hill (Wilts) 30–2
Springfield Lyons (Essex) 40
Sproxton (Leics) 42
Stanford, S.C. 44, 46
Star Carr (Yorks) 14–15
Statute of Merton (AD1250) 128
Stokesay Castle 138

stone circles/rows 35–6
Stow, John 155
Strabo 58
strips (farming) 90
Strixton (Northants) 153
Sutton Hoo Saxon ship burial 7, 96–7
Swanscombe Man 5–6, 9

Tacitus 56, 58, 67
Taylor, Christopher 58–9
Taylor, John 168–9
Thames, River 6
Thetford 110
Thorpe Thewles (Yorks) 53–5
Thwing (Yorks) 40
tin working 39
Tollund Man 56
tools 6, 16–17, 23, 28, 30, 38
Townshend, Charles, 2nd Viscount 173
tree types 14, 53, 58, 107
Troope, Dr 32
Tull, Jethro 180

urban life in mid/late Saxon period 98–101

Viking raids 95–7
villages 80, 84, 89, 110, 116, 118, 145–7

Wallingford (Oxon) 98
Wareham (Dorset) 98
Welsh Annals (tenth century) 76
West Kennet long barrow (Wilts) 32–3, 40
West Stow (Suffolk) 83–4
Wheeler, Sir Mortimer 46, 48
Whittlesford (Cambs) 58
Wildgoose, Martin 59, 130
William of Newburgh 142
William of Normandy, King 103–4, 120
Williams, Michael 129–30
Wilson, Thomas 171
Winchester 98, 110
Windmill Hill (Wilts) 27–33, 48

woodlands 7, 14, 20–1,
  34–5, 52–3, 87–8,
  105–7, 128
 clearance of 20, 29, 38–9,
  54, 99, 101, 125–7,
  154, 168–9
wood pasture (*silva pastilis*)
  107–8, 127
wool production 130, 143,
  145, 154
Wroxeter 62

Yar Tor (Dartmoor) 36
York 61, 98–101, 110, 132,
  155
Young, Arthur 177